SKYRACERS

Table of Contents

SKYRACERS
Matt Watters

SkyRacers is set within the

DREAM PHAZE universe, however, this is a standalone story.

Read
DREAM PHAZE
Germination – Book 1
DREAM PHAZE
Imagination - Book 2
in the continuing series

Chapter One

Another bug splattered and smeared up the cockpit canopy. Its guts and goo seized her attention fleetingly. Aleeza flew dangerously close to the racepod in front. Instinctively, her hand eased up on her throttle for a second. *'Too slow,'* Aleeza thought, *'have to get around it.'*

Aleeza rolled her Formula E-influenced electric racepod right, narrowly missing the small waterfall spilling from the left wall of the narrow gorge. She spotted her air speed out the corner of her eye on the augmented display floating above her control display, *'187 km/h... too slow'*. The Ghost Pod interface displayed her previous, current, and projected position for winning. 'I need to pass!'

The Vikos Gorge sky circuit in Greece was treacherous for SkyRace Grand Prix pilots. Aleeza careened at speed through the narrow river bed, over rapids, barely missing high cliff walls on either side of sweeping bends. A red light flashed on her control display.

'Accident alert, accident alert, rescue vehicle en route,' the Race Traffic Controller warned through her helmet comms system.

Aleeza and several adversaries manoeuvred, jockeying for position, as they navigated the gorge in close proximity, very close proximity to each other. Her MonitoRing glowed on her middle left finger.

'Aleeza, are you alright?' Gordie asked over comms. 'Your vitals aren't good,' the McRory Racing Team Chief continued.

Aleeza's vision blurred, her head throbbed as sensory and physical overload seized control. A momentary lapse of concentration seized her, leading to catastrophic consequences.

'Aleeza, Aleeza! Do you copy?' Gordie demanded.

An almighty crunch triggered Aleeza's adrenalin. Her awareness returned as the cockpit airbags deployed in the blink of an eye. 'Mayday! Mayday, I'm going down.' Aleeza's racepod somersaulted when the damaged front rotors stopped working and the propulsion from the rear rotors drove her end over end. Thumping the ground, momentum tumbled the racepod over and over as angry cracks, scrapes and electronic squeals surrounded her. Blackout.

'Aleeza! Aleeza!' Gordie yelled.

Aleeza blinked repeatedly as her airbags deflated. 'I'm...here, Gordie.' She heard rushing water. Panic set in. She pressed the quick release button on her six-point safety harness, to no avail. She frantically hit the release, but still no luck.

'The chopper's on its way,' Gordie assured her.

She focused beyond a crack in the cockpit canopy at an approaching rescue quadcopter with flashing lights in the distance. 'Copy.' Her vision blurred once more.

Rapid eye movement under Aleeza's eyelids slowed as she regained consciousness. She opened her eyes but remained still for some seconds. The dream was so vivid. It always remained vivid. Under a powder blue sheet on a queen-sized bed, Aleeza contemplated her recurring dream. It would forever etch the 2044 Vikos Gorge crash in her memory.

Aleeza grabbed a couple of iron and vitamin B supplements from her suitcase before she unzipped the entrance in the archway of her inflatable igloo dome. She emerged wearing a colourful skintight designer racesuit carrying her matching helmet. Aleeza Martin was your typical skyracer, toned, and athletic. Her straight, shoulder length auburn hair framed her face. She stood watching, surveying the noisy hive of activity unfolding in front of her. The Texas SkyRace GP was rising from the dirt 70 kilometres southeast of El Paso. She loved to watch the magic of the circus materialise from nothing into an instant, festive township. In a few days, it would vanish as quickly as it arrived.

SkyRace GP infrastructure bump-in was akin to a precision military deployment. Contractors, including techies, tradies, labourers, support crew plus logistic staff, worked to complete their tasks in a specific sequence to the all-important event timetable. An army of people used forklifts and mini cranes to unpack equipment from containers. Quads pulling trailers together with small trucks delivered the parts to their designated locations for assembly. The sky circuit was being digitally mapped and marked with GPS Chronolaser beacons for pilots to follow and be accurately timed. SkyRing International airships were being inflated, the temporary grandstand with seating capacity for 30,000 constructed, inflatable structures and marquees of all shapes and sizes filled, solar power banks assembled, lighting towers erected, massive broadcast wall monitors pieced together, café and bar venues equipped and prepared, portable toilets arranged, amusement rides and dream immersion pods positioned. There was much to do.

SkyRace GP was an extraordinary race series as it needed a 42 kilometre sky circuit away from populated, built-up areas. Away from forests and some waterways because birds and rotor blades don't mix. Each sky circuit location had a unique landscape or challenge for pilots. This rapid staging called for a fleet of land transport to transfer equipment to and from remote event locations. Most equipment was transported by truck, some by helicopter. For that reason, most of the temporary buildings and hangars were inflatables for ease of assembly, storage size, weight and durability. Air was both free and self-transporting. The shipping containers that stored everything doubled as kitchens, offices and workshops. There were four distinct zones, besides the circuit, for the event to take place. Two massive campgrounds for spectators who drove to the event, and another for enthusiasts who flew to the event in their personal cVTOL (electric vertical take-off and landing) aircars. Fresh water, toilet and shower amenities were necessary for both areas. The third zone was the entertainment quarter where the grandstand, cafés, bars, amusement rides, racepod marshalling grid, race team pits and emergency services were located. The last zone was divided into three dedicated areas for race teams, SkyRace GP staff and contractor accommodation, food halls and ablution blocks.

Creating an officially certified pop-up community every three weeks in a different country across 16 events, with all the essential support services, meant event logistics had to be planned down to the smallest detail well in advance. Dedicated legal, environmental and cultural teams liaised with local communities and councils, regional, state, and national government departments. To execute staging with maximum efficiency, they split venue preparation between two identical installation teams. These teams were called Odd and Even. The Odd team serviced events one, three, five and so on, and the Even team serviced events two, four, six, etcetera. Texas was the seventh event of the season, so the Odd team were bumping-in. The day teams and containers arrived to bump-in for SkyRace GP weekends was always Tuesday wherever the circuit was staged in the world. For 72 hours straight, from first light Tuesday morning to first light Friday morning, teams worked around the clock to have everything in place, up and running for circuit practise Friday and spectators.

2048 SkyRace GP Events

GP event	2048 SkyRace GP Events	Date (Sunday)
	Pre-season testing in Chile – closed to the public	9 February
1	Chile	16 February
2	Argentina	8 March
3	Australia	22 March
4	Nigeria	5 April
5	India	19 April
6	Madagascar	10 May
7	USA, El Paso, Texas	31 May
8	Spain	21 June
9	Japan	5 July
10	Canada	26 July
11	Saudi Arabia	16 Aug
12	Egypt	6 Sept
13	Mexico	27 Sept
14	Türkiye	18 Oct
15	South Africa	1 Nov
16	Brazil	15 Nov

Aleeza always flew in on a Tuesday night, earlier than most pilots for race weekends, to watch the spectacle unfold. Many of the 48 pilots opted to stay in 5-star hotels or apartments in the closest city, but not pragmatic Aleeza. Even as the reigning SkyRace GP World Champion, she had her feet planted firmly on the ground, believing her discipline, her regimented routine gave her an edge. Her younger sister liked to get to race meets early for an entirely different reason.

Aleeza walked along a row of identical igloo domes searching for her sister's name, Olivia Martin. Finding it, she touched the name panel, and it buzzed inside. Despite receiving no response, she persisted in touching it again and again. 'I know you're in there,' Aleeza called.

'Go away,' came her muffled instruction.

'I'm coming in,' Aleeza announced before unzipping the entrance and entering. Inside, the dome reeked of alcohol. 'Shit, Olivia. What have you been drinking?' Aleeza left the entry flap wide open, then raised the two window flaps.

'Get out, I'm sleeping.' Olivia was lying sideways across her bed with most of her head under the pillow.

'Get up. We're booked on the racepod simulators at 9:30. You need a shower and we need to eat first.'

'Ten more minutes,' Olivia haggled. 'I didn't get to bed until two...or was it three?'

'You need to stop partying with the crew so late before a race weekend,' Aleeza told her sister.

Olivia snarled, 'As the old saying goes, you do you, I'll do me.' She reluctantly rolled over. Her bottle green hair and eyebrows matched her eyes. Sluggishly, she reached to wipe away crusty eye snot with fingernails matching her hair.

Aleeza and Olivia, both striking women in their designer racesuits, entered Barney's, the race crews' dining hall. The name stuck after the first SkyRace GP tour chef, who was actually a short-order cook. The pair selected breakfast from the bain-marie. SkyRace GP raced on its stomach and pilots were some of the fittest athletes of any sport. They were especially selective with fuel for themselves, making sure they stuck to their personalised dietary plans and never weighed over the strict 75 kilogram limit. For both Aleeza and Olivia, it would be chicken, vegetables, and pasta over the coming days. Red meat was a no go until after their races. A few high-profile pilots travelled with their own chefs to cater for quite specific dietary requirements and never set foot in Barney's.

After breakfast, Olivia and Aleeza headed to the racepod simulation marquee to practise. Since it was Wednesday, the tech crews were still assembling and inspecting their racepods. They wouldn't be flight-ready until tomorrow morning when both Division 1 (D1) and Division 2 (D2) pilots had to be onsite for testing. Four Reality XLR8 full flight D1 and four Reality XLR8 full flight D2 racepod simulators sat assembled and ready in the marquee.

Olivia was the #1 pilot for McRory Racing D2 team. All D2 pilots flew identical electric racepods from Kobe Advanced Rotor Aeronautics (KARA), the Edge V5 model. They were less powerful than the D1 customised, high performance racepods. Aleeza was the #1 pilot for McRory Racing D1 team. Both women had extensive aviation backgrounds with multi-rotor aircraft and both had graduated from the SkyRace Pilot Academy with a SkyRace GP Pilot Licence. Olivia was previously a helicopter test pilot, an air ambulance helicopter pilot and helicopter tour pilot in British Columbia servicing high altitude tourist destinations. Aleeza joined the Royal Canadian Air Force at 18 and trained as a helicopter pilot. She then joined Search and Rescue British Columbia as a helicopter pilot, even flying water bomber choppers during wildfires.

A SkyRace racepod, officially known as a rotorcraft octocopter, had four sets of dual coaxial rotors. Two sets were in front and two sets at the rear, all working independently of each other. This configuration gave racepods maximum manoeuvrability at high speed. The D1 racepods had additional propulsion, a ducted air intake bladeless thruster embedded in the airframe's rear, which meant they required a larger Graphene Biolyte NF (non-flammable) battery. All racepod fuselages were virtually indestructible, made from graphene-reinforced carbon fibre composite monocoque construction.

'I'm going to try a D1 simulator today,' Olivia announced. 'Want to race?' she challenged her sister.

'Are you up to it after last night?'

Olivia laughed. 'I'll knock you off your perch.'

'If you say so,' Aleeza agreed.

Both pilots donned their open-faced helmets before walking separate narrow gangplanks to enter a spherical D1 racepod simulator. The gangplank automatically retracted as the simulator door slide closed and locked. The simulator sat atop a fluid motion octaline system, which provided unfettered freedom of movement in all directions. Inside each sphere, they were fitted out to resemble a D1 racepod cockpit in every detail. They both climbed into the cockpit and fitted the safety harness. Once the sixth harness clip clicked into the centre buckle, the canopy closed and the magic began. The interior surface of the entire sphere changed to a quicksilver grey fluid, seamlessly transporting the pair of racepods to an open field sitting side by side on a sun-drenched day.

'Have you got a circuit preference?' Aleeza asked Olivia.

'Let's go home. What about the short circuit west of Calgary?'

'Sure. Simulator, Canadian short circuit.'

The simulator virtually relocated them to the sky circuit west of Calgary, Alberta. A 360 degree vista surrounded them as they engaged engines, initiated flight control displays and ascended towards the start-finish line. They hovered side-by-side in pole position ten metres off the ground. In front of them, augmented rectangular guidance grids projected into the distance, plotting the sky circuit.

'Good to go. Start sequence in 3-2-1,' Aleeza forewarned. Red lights on either side of the start line lit up one by one from bottom to top, then after a pause, lights off, signifying the start of the race.

Aleeza got the jump on Olivia by 0.2 of a second and immediately ascended, while Olivia maintained her altitude, getting a feel for the racepod.

After the race, the pair exited the simulators. Zetta Minn, #2 pilot in Division 1 for the Lazzrini Race Team, was waiting for her turn.

'I was watching the monitors. Impressive, Olivia. That was damn good racing. You almost had her,' Zetta complimented.

'She'll retire a D2 winner at best,' Aleeza mocked her sister with a cheeky grin.

'If I wasn't under the weather, I would have beaten you.'

'That would be a first,' Aleeza teased.

'Got a bug?' Zetta queried with concern.

'Yep, the type of bug found at the bottom of a mezcal bottle,' Aleeza remarked. 'Is Marco here yet?' she asked Zetta.

'Haven't seen him. Probably sleeping in as usual.'

'Speaking of sleep, that's where I'm going,' Olivia informed them on her way out.

'I'm going for a 15-minute run,' Aleeza told Zetta. 'See you.'

After testing and calibrating onboard flight and tracking systems with pit crew all Thursday, the 12 SkyRace GP race teams were halfway through circuit practise on Friday. Every race team had a #1 and #2 pilot in both Division 1 and 2, totalling 48 pilots. D2 pilots had circuit practise starting at 8:30am, leaving at five-minute intervals to traverse the 42 kilometre sky circuit to work out where the nuances and problems may lie. All 24 D2 pilots could fly two practise laps before lunch. After lunch, the D1 pilots were going through the same practise procedure but flying racepods with more grunt.

Spectators and aficionados arrived from all corners of the globe early Friday morning by traditional car, RV, aircars and charter buses carrying international visitors from El Paso International Airport. The 42-kilometre circuit provided numerous vantage points for camping enthusiasts to claim their spot for the D2 race on Saturday and the D1 race on Sunday. The series had established a solid, family-friendly entertainment atmosphere that didn't stop when the races did. Cafés, amusement rides, a VRXLR8 complex, live bands, ILM Holo-array 3D movies projected in the night sky, and synchronised micro-drone light shows catered to all tastes. This event formula had added massive value to the entertainment experience economy and kept crowds captivated and coming back for more.

Rumours rapidly swirled during practise within the tight-knit SkyRace GP community about the missing #1 pilot for the Lazzrini Race Team, Marco Franks. He didn't show up for the compulsory practice session, and his team reported they hadn't heard from him.

Spirits were high in the McRory Racing hangar. Olivia did well during her practise session as did Aleeza, being one of the early D1 pilots to complete her laps. The teams timed their practise laps, while pilots focused on getting a feel for the circuit's peculiarities.

'If you can improve on that time in the sprint qualifying session by a few seconds Sunday, you'll be close to poll,' Gordie told Aleeza.

'The horn always catches me off guard.' Aleeza complained. From above on the circuit map, the very western point of the circuit resembled a rhino horn, a hairpin right bend difficult to navigate. 'I think it's the closeness of the cliff walls on that acute turn. The other hairpins are in open space. I felt the same last year too.'

Gordie considered her. 'Could it be trauma from your Vikos Gorge crash in Greece?'

Aleeza studied Gordie's weathered face. 'I didn't think of that. You know, you might be right.'

'No one has seen Marco yet,' Olivia mentioned, sidling up to Aleeza. 'There's a rumour you had him detained,' she laughed.

'Who the fuck said that?'

'Guess,' one of the pit crew hissed as he joined them. Dylan, a mid-twenty-something, gestured to his right.

Aleeza followed his gaze. 'De Castro.'

At that moment, Lukas de Castro, the #1 pilot in Division 1 for Eagle One Racing, and Aleeza's nemesis, caught Aleeza's eye. The 34-year-old Brazilian couldn't help himself and sauntered over to the McRory Racing hangar with his female entourage in tow. The three statuesque Amazon women accompanying Lukas de Castro were adorned with multiple facial tattoos, piercings and all sported the latest fashion craze, opalised rainbow flecked eyes.

'So, there's a rumour you had Marco Franks detained at the airport to have a better chance Sunday.'

'I wonder what sort of cockroach would circulate such gossip, Lukas. Believe me, if I had the power to detain anyone, it would be you,' Aleeza hit back with a smile.

'Come Sunday, you will have wished you did because I'm going to crush you, Martin.'

'The buzz around the pits is that you pay these girls to hang around because you couldn't satisfy them with that,' Olivia teased, pointing to his crotch with her little finger and wiggling it. 'You don't look like you pack much of a punch down there.'

Dylan and one of Lukas' girls sniggered at her remark.

Lukas shot the woman beside him a scorching glare. His manhood was noticeably dressed to the left in his custom-fitted Flomex fireproof racesuit. Some of the woven suit patterns evoked a superhero appearance. Unfortunately, not for Lukas.

'You'll never get to find out, Martin #2,' Lukas scoffed as he walked away with his herd.

'Arsehole,' Olivia uttered under her breath. 'You'd better beat him on Sunday.'

'I'll do my best,' Aleeza responded.

A SkyRing International airship, tethered 400 metres above the start/ finish line, was a premium vantage point to watch the races. The SkyRing airship, as the name implied, was a torus or doughnut shape. They had electric stabilising engines but flew nowhere, just ascended and descended. The viewing gondola, also circular shaped, hung suspended below the blimp and accommodated an exclusive bar and buffet for 120 VIP guests. Mounted underneath the viewing gondola were a series of ARRI Eagle Eye stabilised ground-controlled cameras for unequalled live broadcasting by the Sports Entertainment Network

(SEN). They strategically positioned six SkyRing International airships around the circuit for extensive coverage along the entire 42 kilometres.

'...SkyRace GP has become a worldwide juggernaut on the sporting calendar with massive media interest since I last pulled on a racesuit six years ago,' Katie Kang, the SEN sportscaster remarked, as her image replaced the vision of racepods on wall screens broadcast from the airship mounted cameras. The broadcast feed played across multiple wall screens positioned around the entertainment quarter. It fed her voice through spectators' Personal Devices (PD) so it didn't interfere with race announcements. 'The series has generated a river of gold for the Deltop Media Group since taking control of the commercial rights to the SkyRace GP World Championship in '43, with an average worldwide audience per race of about 130 million viewers. I remember Deltop Media Group's chairperson and largest shareholder, the recluse Ted Pearl, saying it was the best billion-dollar investment he ever made. We're going to cross to Harvie Stedman who is on pitpad with a very special guest. Harvie.'

'Thanks, Katie, I have the #1 skyracer in the world with me, SkyRace GP Division 1 World Champion Aleeza Martin. Aleeza, this year is going well for you so far. You won the last race in Madagascar and you're sitting at the top of the pilot standings after six races. Has this year been more hectic, with more expectations since becoming the World Champion?'

'Usually, my working year is about ten percent flying, the rest is travel, marketing and media. There is definitely more marketing and media this year.'

'I believe your endorsements have increased substantially since becoming the face of the sport. It must be exhausting?'

'It can be. I didn't appreciate, and I don't think some of our fans and spectators realise just how much work goes on outside the racepods. I'm lucky enough to glimpse the internal operations, the equipment logistics, the workforce logistics and the financial side of

SkyRacing. It is a mammoth task to take this event around the globe, event after event, year after year, and I'm so proud to be part of such a huge sporting machine.'

'Besides being in front of more cameras, has becoming World Champion changed your life?'

'Flying for McRory has given me unimaginable opportunities. Opportunities I thought I would never have. I love flying and I see this job as a privileged lifestyle.'

'A lifestyle that pays well,' Harvie joked.

'It does,' Aleeza agreed. 'And I say to any junior pilots watching, you can be part of this if you train hard and have the drive to turn your dreams into reality.'

'Thank you for speaking with me, Aleeza, and good luck on Sunday.'

'Thanks, Harvie.'

As Aleeza walked away, Lukas de Castro snaked his way towards the camera and microphone from behind her for an impromptu interview.

'Hello, Harvie.'

'Ah, erm... Lukas, we have, we have Lukas de Castro from the Eagle One Racing team with us,' Harvie stumbled.

'Hello, Harvie,' Lukas repeated, flashing a huge smile for the camera.

'Lukas, Aleeza won in Madagascar and you're currently trailing Aleeza Martin in the points standings—'

'By a mere 11 points, Harvie. Sunday I'll probably be on top of the standings.'

'So your plan is to finish top five to snatch the lead?'

'I'll probably win on Sunday, Harvie,' he boasted.

'You haven't won this season. Aleeza has won twice. Do you think Sunday might be your turn?'

'I've had two podium finishes, second and third, so I'm due for a win. Sunday will be my win.'

'You were World Champion in '45, Lazzrini's Marco Franks won in '46 and Aleeza Martin took home the crown last year. Do you think you've still got what it takes to be World Champion?'

'Yes, Harvie. SkyRacing is my life. It has given me everything. Because of SkyRacing, I own several houses, a superyacht, a garage full of custom flycycles and aircars, a light-aircraft and a helicopter. I have done very well for myself and I'm not finished yet.'

'Thank you, Lukas, and good luck on Sunday. Back to you, Katie.'

When Lukas knew the broadcast feed cut, he grabbed Harvie by the arm. 'What the fuck was that? You made me look like an over the hill loser.'

'Get your hand off me, Lukas,' the Nigerian born commentator, who was beefier than Lukas, threatened. 'You are a loser, Lukas. You weaselled your way into an interview and then bragged about all your fucking toys like a child. In future, get Mariela or Katie to interview you. I won't.' Harvie dashed off after another pilot.

When Aleeza got back to the McRory hangar, Olivia was speaking to their father, Nicolas Martin, on her Personal Device. His holographic image projected from her PD.

'Dad!' Aleeza greeted as she stood next to her sister. 'Are you here, in El Paso?'

'Just flew in. Grabbed a courtesy jump seat on a Delta from LAX. I'll check-in and be there soon.'

'Are you flying here or driving?' Olivia asked.

'I fly for a living like you two. I've got a rental so I can enjoy the scenery.'

'Mum's birthday tomorrow,' Olivia reminded him with a tinge of sadness.

Aleeza put her arm around Olivia's shoulder. 'I think Dad remembers.'

'I remembered,' Nicolas responded. 'I see her in both of you every time I look at you.'

'See you soon,' Olivia disconnected before the emotion got too raw.

'You okay?' Aleeza asked her sister. Olivia nodded. The sisters wandered over to some of the crew who stood around a TV monitor. 'What's happening?'

'They found Marco Franks in a ditch,' Gordie answered.

'Shush,' Olivia instructed.

'...he failed to arrive for his scheduled flight on Wednesday morning after breaking his leg in a motorcycle accident just outside Dublin in Ireland the night before,' the news reporter explained. 'He was supposed to be competing in the SkyRace GP in El Paso, Texas this weekend.' Rough night footage showed the motorcycle in a ditch down an embankment on a desolate stretch of road. 'They found Marco Franks in this ditch by the side of the road late Friday.'

'No wonder they couldn't find him,' Brad Hazzard commented.

'Brad! Cleared for 15 minutes. Let's go,' Dylan yelled from across the hangar.

'Good luck,' Aleeza wished her #2 pilot for his practise session. 'Buy you a Crew Juice tonight if you beat my time.'

'Two.'

'I'll buy you three,' she agreed with a smile. 'I know I'm safe.'

'Brad,' Gordie placed his arm around Brad's shoulders as if he was about to divulge a secret and led him away. 'I want you to concentrate on...'

'Poor Marco,' Aleeza lamented.

Olivia stared at her sister with a wicked smirk. 'Couldn't have planned it any better if you tried.'

'Shut up!' Aleeza gently shoved her. 'Marco is probably lying in a hospital bed in Ireland and you, evil sister, are making jokes.'

'I'll tell Lukas he should be scared, very scared.' They laughed.

'I need a nap before tonight,' Aleeza uttered as she grabbed her helmet. 'See you there.'

Several hours later, the festival was in full swing in the entertainment quarter. The family-friendly atmosphere attracted attendees from the surrounding campgrounds like gnats to a porch light as the sky ignited with holograms and light drones. The SkyRing airship was lit up and blazoned with advertising from one of the major sponsors, Bent Sprocket Beer.

At the customary Friday night pre-race function at Rohlfs Bar, pilots, team crews and invited guests had gathered. Aleeza and Olivia sat chatting with their father.

'So, is Marco out for the year?' Nicolas asked the pair.

'We don't know. How long does it take for a leg to mend?' Olivia questioned.

'Months I would imagine, so he might be back,' Aleeza guessed.

'I broke my leg back in 2008 horse-riding,' Nicolas told them. 'Damn thing bolted, and I fell off and landed sideways on a fallen tree. That took three months to heal completely, so he could return before the end of the season.'

Brad Hazzard sat down at their table. 'How are you, Nicolas?'

'Terrible.'

Brad looked at Aleeza and Olivia for some clue to the issue. 'Sorry to hear that. May I ask what's wrong?'

'Nothing. But if I said I was good, you wouldn't have given me a second thought. This way there is a bit of interest and a brief interaction.'

Brad smiled. 'So, how is Air Canada treating you, Nicolas?' Brad thought he would keep the interest going.

'Glad you asked. An aircraft jet engine ingested a rookie ramp worker as it taxied towards a gate in Toronto yesterday.'

'That's terrible,' Brad remarked. 'You don't walk away from that.'

'Nope. Just three days on the job. Other than that, same old same old. Pilot staffing issues, so I'm working more flights. Furious customers over flight cancellations due to fleet maintenance problems, and they tried to cancel my leave for this weekend and roster me on, but because I'm a minor celebrity in the organisation because of these two, I pushed back.' They all laughed at his audacity.

'Glad you did,' Brad agreed. 'Speaking of daughters, my two want a photo with you two tomorrow.'

'Of course,' Aleeza agreed, as Olivia nodded.

'How old are Klara and... ' Nicolas began but couldn't remember.

'Amalia,' Brad finished. 'Klara is seven and Amalia is ten.'

'That's right, same age difference between these two, 29 and 32,' Nicolas remembered.

Brad turned to Aleeza. 'You owe me a drink or three.'

'Bullshit! You didn't beat my time, I asked Gordie.'

'Shit, I was hoping to get to you before he did,' Brad admitted.

'I'll buy you one anyway. Come on.' They got up and headed to the bar.

Nicolas looked over at Olivia. 'Your mother would have turned 56 tomorrow.'

'Yep.' Olivia swished her beverage around in her glass. Olivia was only 14 when her mother died from cancer at 41. 'Live life today, tomorrow is only a promise.'

'Do you still have the tattoo?' her father asked. 'I know you had some removed.' Olivia pulled up her left sleeve and showed her inked inside forearm. 'I remember when you got that. The day after your 18th birthday, because it was a Sunday, the same day they issued your helicopter pilot licence.'

'I don't know how many times she said that to me in her last six months,' Olivia reminisced.

'Suzanne would be so proud of her girls.'

Olivia smiled. 'I'd like to think so.'

Zetta Minn approached their table. 'Hi, Nicolas.'

'Hello, Zetta. Shame about Marco.'

'Yeah, it came as a shock.'

'How's your daughter going? What's her name, Anna?'

'Andrea. Great. She started school this year. Natasha, my partner, wanted to home school her, but Italian schools provide excellent support for children on the autism spectrum, so she loves it.' Zetta looked at Olivia. 'Can I have a word? Can I steal this one for a quick word?' she asked Nicolas.

Nicolas glanced at Olivia, then back to Zetta. 'Of course, sure.'

Olivia followed Zetta over to a table where Lazzrini Race Team Principal Sergio Pirozzi sat.

Aleeza and Brad returned to the table with drinks in hand. 'Here you go, Dad. We'll have a toast to Mum. Where's Olivia?' Her father pointed to the table where Zetta, Sergio, and Olivia met talking.

'What's that all about?' Brad wondered.

'Marco is out for the entire season?' Olivia repeated in amazement.

'His right knee was crushed. He'll need a knee replacement and months of physiotherapy to get him back on his feet,' Sergio confirmed. 'Zetta will move up to #1 pilot for our team on Sunday. Now please hear me out with what I'm about to say. I want to offer you the #2 pilot position on our D1 team if you win tomorrow.'

Olivia didn't react at first, looking from Sergio to Zetta to Sergio and back to Zetta. 'Is he serious?'

'Quite serious. We think you're the right pilot to fill the spot.'

Olivia laughed. 'You're out of your mind. I fly for McRory! I fly Division 2. I would have to–'

'Win tomorrow,' Zetta finished. 'We know. If you win tomorrow, the rules stipulate for a Division 2 pilot outside the team to replace an ill or missing Division 1 pilot at a current race meet, there has to be an offer made from the impeded team and then you can fill it and fly Sunday.'

Olivia sat silent for a long moment, her inner monologue racing. 'Why aren't you promoting your D2 pilots, erm... Nino Lombardi or Roselyn Nash?'

'In all honesty, Olivia,' Sergio continued. 'They are excellent pilots, but Nino is in 10th place and Roselyn 14th on the pilot standings. Neither has won this season and we don't think they are ready to handle the power of a D1 racepod. You, on the other hand, have had podium finishes in your last three races, winning in Chile.'

'What about Takata Jun?' Olivia countered. 'He's at the top of the standings, or, or Damian Rosser in second place?'

'Takata has just signed a new two-year contract with Hoverflyers, and Damian hasn't won this year. Second is his best,' Zetta answered. 'I watched you almost beat Aleeza Wednesday morning–'

'In a simulator for fuck's sake!'

'Yes, but I've been paying attention, Olivia. You have superb piloting skills. You almost beat Aleeza in the simulator because you concentrate on strategy and that impressed me. How should I put it? Some pilots are born with remarkable instinct, some with the required strategy and ambition to win, then there are unique pilots who have all these and that pushes them to a new level, to know when to take risks and when to back off and bide their time to achieve a win. Aleeza is a skilful skyracer with instinct and strategy, and I also think you are.'

Olivia looked across at her sister, father and Brad sitting at the table chatting. 'I think it's in our family's DNA,' she replied, softly touching her left forearm.

'I think so,' Zetta agreed.

'Lazzrini doesn't have an experienced D1 pilot in the US to replace Marco,' Sergio explained. 'We will lose significant team points. We know you can handle the powerful D1 racepods.'

'I can't just walk away from McRory mid-season.'

'McRory has access to a pool of pilots that could replace you in D2 from the feeder Division 3 and 4 ranks. Bottom line, Olivia, the dream I'm selling is opportunity,' Sergio tempted, 'the opportunity to move up and compete with the best pilots in the competition, in the top division. We know you come off contract at the end of the season. We will offer you a significant package, including a substantial salary increase, a one year contract to start with and an option for a further year. There is also the opportunity for more lucrative endorsements from global brands.'

Across the room, Aleeza watched the engaged trio's conversation with interest. 'What do you think they're talking about, Brad?'

Brad turned his attention to the group. 'Are they pitching for a pilot?'

His observation took Aleeza by surprise. She looked across at her father, who was listening. He raised his eyebrows as he sipped his beer.

'I won't lie. This would be my dream job,' Olivia admitted to the pair. 'But, I thought it would be with McRory.'

'Not while Aleeza and Brad Hazzard are there,' Sergio prodded. 'You must think about your career, Olivia.'

Olivia stared at the two of them. 'Is this only about team points? Marco had issues in the last race in Madagascar and didn't finish. So no points.'

Zetta gave Sergio an uneasy look. 'As we are all being honest. That is our motivation. But as Sergio said, this is a golden opportunity for you, Olivia. You know the Lazzrini Race Team is currently second on points, behind McRory, and winning pays far better than second. But this conversation means nothing unless you win tomorrow.'

'True,' Olivia concurred. 'I'll consider the offer... if I win.'

'All we ask is you keep this conversation to yourself for now,' Sergio requested. 'We don't want the media knowing there was an offer at this point in time.'

Olivia nodded in agreement.

A short time later, Aleeza asked Olivia about the conversation with Zetta and Sergio.

'Well, I can't...I can't really talk about it,' she answered awkwardly.

'What? What was the conversation about?'

Olivia grabbed her sister's arm and pulled her into an area secluded by plants. 'I'll only tell you if you promise me not to tell anyone. This is 100 percent confidential,' she stressed.

'Is this about Marco?' Aleeza questioned.

'In some respects, yes.'

Aleeza studied her sister. 'In some respects? Tell me what you spoke about.'

'Only if you promise not to discuss what I tell you with another human being,' Olivia spelt out.

'Okay.'

'Okay what?'

'I promise not to discuss what you tell me with another human being.'

Olivia spent the next few minutes outlining the proposition pitched by Zetta and Sergio.

'I can't believe what you just told me. You can't do it! Point-blank, even if you win tomorrow, you can't do it,' Aleeza told her sister. 'It would be a slap in the face for Gordie and the entire team to leave them high and dry mid-season. Look at them over there.' She pointed towards the McRory crew table, enjoying the night. 'These people have taken you on as a rookie, paid you a truckload of money, and now you're going to jump ship mid-season.'

'I'm not a rookie. This is my second season. We have actual rookie pilots who could replace me in a heartbeat from Division 3.'

'It's not good optics during a race meet for you, for the McRory team, to up and fuck off to the competition!' Aleeza stressed. 'Fuck! Do you understand the media would eat you alive?'

Olivia felt anxious by Aleeza's unexpected reaction. 'I have to think about my career, Aleeza.'

'This is not the way to advance your career. This is not an opportunity. They are playing you to maintain their team standing. This is all about money at the end of the season for the Lazzrini Race Team.'

'It's win-win.'

Aleeza threw her hands in the air. 'You can't do this, Olivia. You just can't do it.'

'You can't tell me what to do anymore, Aleeza. It's my life, my choice. I'm not that naïve little sister you used to manipulate.'

'What?' Aleeza asked, wearing a puzzled expression. 'What are you talking about? What does that even mean?'

'You know what that means.' Olivia stormed off towards the bar.

Brad wandered over to Aleeza after the confrontation. 'What was that all about?'

Aleeza was not in the frame of mind to discuss anything. 'I'm not sure yet.'

Chapter Two

Aleeza woke in the middle of the night in a sweat. She went to the mini fridge and got out a jug of water and poured herself a glass. She sat outside under the stars, thinking.

Early next morning, Jericho Starling, the McRory Racing Team Principal, tapped repeatedly on Olivia's name plate outside her igloo dome, making it buzz inside. Gordie, Aleeza, and Brad were with him, waiting for a response.

'Go away, I'm sleeping.'

'Olivia, it's Jericho Starling. I need to speak to you urgently.'

Olivia sluggishly made her way to the archway and unzipped the entry flap enough to stick her head out. She squinted through half-closed eyes and saw Jericho, Aleeza, Gordie and Brad staring back at her.

'What the fuck, Olivia!' Gordie challenged.

'We need to talk now,' Jericho demanded. 'Can we come in?' He unzipped the rest of the flap and pushed past her before she granted permission. The others filed in behind him. Olivia glared at Aleeza as she pushed past her in the narrow entrance.

Aleeza didn't waste any time. 'I slept little last night, worried about what you told me. I've told them.'

'Obviously. A dissolving promise, was it?' Olivia walked over and sat on the bed while the four stood self-consciously around it in the confined space. She scrutinised each of them. 'I feel this is a little premature, considering I have to win for any of this to happen.'

'Are you really considering this?' Gordie questioned.

'Look, Gordie, I listened to Zetta and Sergio's proposal. I told them I'd consider it. End of story.'

'Not end of story, Olivia!' Jericho screamed. 'SkyRace GP is a team sport, not a solo sport. You wouldn't be flying in the most watched sport on the planet if it wasn't for this team around you. Us!'

'Flying for Lazzrini is not a promotion, it's a demotion,' Gordie chimed in. 'McRory is the best team in the competition and that's reflected in our points and position. We are number one.'

'If you move to Lazzrini, it will leave McRory weak, drastically impacting our team points because we have to break in a Division 3 rookie mid-season,' Brad added.

'It takes time to be good enough in D1 to become the World Champion. It's taken the team and Aleeza five years to do it. If you stay with the team, we'll do the same for you.' Jericho offered an olive branch.

'I will never get a chance to fly D1 while Brad and Aleeza are flying for McRory. This is my opportunity to advance my career.' No one had a reply to her assertion. Olivia seized the moment. 'Although... there is a solution.'

'What?' Gordie jumped in.

'My contract, and Brad's, are both up at the end of this season. Sign me for another two years today, before the race, as a D1 pilot and I won't give it another thought.'

'Fuck you!' Brad scoffed. 'She's suffering from gratitude deficit syndrome. You're thinking of yourself again and not the team.'

Olivia looked at Jericho, and everyone followed her gaze. 'Well?'

Jericho grunted and turned away. 'I don't control the purse strings. I run the team. A new deal mid-season isn't my call.'

'So, who can make that deal?' Olivia pushed.

Jericho looked at Gordie before he spoke. 'Mason-Stuart. Paul Mason-Stuart can make that call.'

'Okay, you call Paul and I'll wait for your answer,' Olivia told him.

'Now wait on, Jericho,' Brad piped up. 'I was given verbal assurance McRory would contract me for next year.'

'By who?' Olivia asked.

Brad looked uncomfortable before he replied. 'Gordie.'

They stood in silence until Olivia laughed. 'Well, Brad, I don't think Gordie's verbal assurance carries much sway if his boss can't make that call. Right, Jericho? Now, if you would all like to fuck off, I have a sprint qualifying session I have to get ready for.'

Gordie, Brad, and Jericho shuffled out, leaving Aleeza. 'I hope you know what you're doing, Olivia, because if you don't, you'll crash and burn everyone around you.'

'That sounds ominous.'

'It's reality. SkyRacing is about money, not big money, massive money. That means it's a cutthroat business. Just make sure it's not your throat.'

An hour later, after Olivia had called her father, they met at one of the cafés in the entertainment quarter.

'Have you spoken to Aleeza since last night?' Olivia asked her father.

'No. Why?'

Olivia explained her conversation with Zetta and Sergio last night and the confrontation earlier this morning. 'I don't know what to do, Dad.'

'Wait until you speak to Jericho. He might surprise you and offer you a two-year contract. You're a damn fine pilot.'

'I doubt it. This is only my second year in D2 and Brad is an experienced pilot with a solid race record.'

Nicolas took his daughter's hand. 'We humans are complex beings. What do *you* want? Is your heart conflicted with the possibility of leaving McRory and going up against Aleeza, Brad and the team? Or is your internal dialogue sprinting, debating the what ifs? Is your gut screaming, go for it, see what happens? Only you know the answers to those questions.'

Olivia looked at her father. 'All of what you said is happening inside me. I'm confused. Then, on top of all this, it's happening on Mum's birthday.'

'You think it might be a sign?' Nicolas questioned.

'No, no, nothing like that,' she snorted. 'I'm not superstitious. There are just too many things converging today. I was looking forward to spending some time with you over the weekend on Mum's birthday.'

'We still can.'

'Sure, but things might be different by the end of today.'

'If Jericho says no, you have to make a hard decision if you win today. But process it logically, with the information at hand.'

'What would Mum say to me given the circumstances?'

'See what Jericho says, then take it from there. Make one decision at a time based on the information.'

'Same as you.'

He smiled. 'We were usually in sync.'

A short time later, Aleeza watched Jericho, Gordy and Olivia in conversation on the other side of the McRory hangar. Olivia's dejected body language told her all she needed to know.

'Doesn't look like they offered her a contract,' Brad commented as he walked up beside Aleeza.

'No,' she replied flatly. 'The day just got a lot more complicated.'

Olivia slipped out of the McRory hangar and found Zetta in the Lazzrini hangar and gestured to follow her outside. 'I just want to confirm the offer still stands.'

'Yes,' Zetta affirmed softly. 'But there is a complication.'

'What?'

'Our Team Chief, Henri Rossi, wants a meeting with you before the deal is done.'

'Does he have to give his stamp of approval?'

'He would like to think so,' Zetta commented. 'He can be a hothead sometimes.'

'What about right now?' Olivia took the initiative.

'Now?' Zetta thought for a moment. 'Give me a minute.' Zetta disappeared back into the Lazzrini hangar. A few minutes later, she returned with Sergio Pirozzi and Henri Rossi. 'Olivia, this is Henri, our Team Chief.'

'Pleased to meet you, Henri.' Olivia confidently offered her hand. 'I've seen you around, but I don't believe we've ever met.'

Henri Rossi, a striking, blue-eyed Northern Italian in his mid-30s, looked down at her hand but did not reciprocate. 'Why are you defecting from McRory mid-season?'

His question offended Olivia. 'I'm not defecting, as you put it. You need a pilot and I'm hoping to advance my career.'

'No, I am not in favour of this arrangement. I do not feel you are ready for D1. I think we should give Nino the chance before you.'

'Henri, we spoke about this,' Sergio berated. 'Nino isn't ready to fly D1.'

'I do not agree. Give him a chance over this defector,' Henri insolently responded to his boss.

'I'm not a defector!' Olivia asserted to Henri. 'I, I don't know if I want to work with this arsehole,' she told Sergio and Zetta. 'I have to go.'

'Olivia!' Zetta called after her. She turned to Henri. 'She is correct. You are an arsehole.'

'If Olivia wins, it will be your job to secure her for the Lazzrini team,' Sergio Pirozzi told Henri matter-of-factly. 'If you don't,' Sergio poked his index finger sharply into Henri's chest, 'you will look for another job. Exceptional pilots are rare. I can replace you. The success of this team is more important than your fucking ego and friendships.'

Zetta shot Henri a filthy look before she returned to the Lazzrini hangar.

In the McRory hangar, still irritated by her meeting with the Lazzrini team, Olivia tried to concentrate and prepare for the sprint qualifying session.

Shortly after, a high-pitched squeal echoed through the hangar, and Brad's daughters hurried over to wrap their arms around his waist while his wife followed closely behind.

'I couldn't keep them away any longer,' she admitted.

'Hi, Astrid,' Aleeza welcomed.

'How are you, Aleeza?'

As Aleeza was about to speak, Klara and Amalia hugged her from both sides, interrupting her. 'Wow, you two have grown since I last saw you!' Aleeza exclaimed.

'We want to get a photo with you and Olivia,' Amalia gushed.

'Of course. Now?'

'Now, now, now!' Klara repeated at volume.

Brad looked at Aleeza with concern. 'Maybe we should wait—'

'Hi, girls!' Olivia called to them with enthusiasm.

'Olivia!' Klara shrieked as Olivia picked her up and twirled around. 'Can we have a photo with you and Aleeza?'

'Of course,' she responded. 'Come on, Amalia, let's get a photo.' Olivia walked over to Aleeza. 'Ready?'

'Sure.' The two stood shoulder to shoulder. Klara stood in front of Olivia. 'Come on, Amalia.' The young girl positioned herself in front of Aleeza.

Astrid had her PD in hand, ready. 'Keep still, Klara. Okay, say cheese.' The group complied.

From across the hangar, Dylan called out. 'Olivia cleared for 15 minutes. Time to go.'

'I have to get ready. I'm up.'

Brad and his family wished her luck as she walked away.

'Olivia,' Aleeza touched her arm. 'It took me three years to break into Division 1–'

'I know, because of the Greece crash.'

'Olivia!' Dylan called to her again.

'I have to go.' Olivia left Aleeza.

A couple of hours later, the SkyRace GP Division 2 race was an hour from starting. Cameras on SkyRing blimps broadcast footage to the grandstand wall screens of random groups of fans with the best vantage points around the circuit. Most sat on camp chairs around barbecues with drinks in hand.

Vision on the wall screens swapped to drone shots from the start grid 30-minute walk through by spectators and media. The SkyRace GP start grid was a transportable rubber sheet. They made the physical grid with interlocking rubber tiles that formed the sheet, stretching across the 30 metre width of the circuit, and along for 80 metres. Rotors generate a lot of dust from downward thrust, especially in the desert, and the dust minimisation grid sheet made life easier for pilots, crew, race officials and spectators. They divided the grid sheet into 24 start squares, three across and eight deep, each measuring ten by ten metres. The three fastest pilots in the sprint qualifying session garnered pole position, followed by the 21 remaining pilots. The walk through was intimidating, hectic and brisk for both spectators and pilots. Superfans jockeyed for position for selfies with their idols and team racepods.

Olivia turned in a solid performance in sprint qualifying, clocking the fourth fastest time and would start in the second row on the grid.

Klara ran to Olivia and hugged her as Amalia followed with Astrid behind. 'I know you'll win, Olivia.'

'Good luck, Olivia,' Astrid encouraged.

'Thanks. I'm a little off pole, but I can make it up.'

Further down the start grid, Brad Hazzard finished a discussion with Max Schroder, McRory's #2 pilot in the race, and both the Lazzrini team pilots, Roselyn Nash and Nino Lombardi. He made his way towards his family and Olivia's racepod. Klara and Amalia were getting another photo with Olivia next to her racepod as he arrived.

'Come on, let's leave Olivia to get ready.'

'Good luck, Olivia. Win for me!' Klara called.

Brad slipped Olivia a sideways smile as he herded Klara and his family off the start grid.

Nicolas Martin and Aleeza approached Olivia and waited as enthusiastic fans took photos with her and she signed their merchandise. When they left, the pair seized the opportunity for a quick family confab.

'Just do your best,' Aleeza encouraged her sister. 'Focus on the task at hand.'

'Whatever happens today, your mother would be proud,' Nicolas assured his daughter. 'Fly like no one is watching.'

Before Olivia could say anything, the announcement came over the event speakers to clear the grid for scrutineering before the start of the race. Both Aleeza and her father gave Olivia a quick hug of support before they headed off the grid as race officials entered to begin their inspections.

The rules were simple; the pilot who crossed the finish line first after completing the pre-determined number of laps was declared the winner. SkyRace GP used a three dimensional start grid formation. Pole position racepods started ten metres off the ground with the following seven rows at 15, 20, 25 metres, etcetera, up to 45 metres altitude. This gave all pilots space and the best chance of not colliding during the start. From the rear of the grid, team safety crews cautiously guided their pilots vertically into position from their start grid square.

'Pilots ready,' came the priming announcement over the event speakers and simultaneously in all pilot helmets.

Two banks of five red lights, suspended 20 metres off the ground on either side at the front of the grid, lit up one by one from bottom to top, then after a pause, lights off, signalling the start of the race. Like a mechanised swarm of ravenous wasps, every racepod accelerated, accompanied by their familiar high-pitched whine.

Olivia's adrenaline pumped as pilots jostled for position. The start of any SkyRace GP was the most nerve-racking, as information immediately flooded the cockpit from onboard and external systems. LiDAR (Light imaging, Detection, And Ranging), MVT (Machine Vision Technology), RADAR and GPS collision avoidance systems, combined to create an avalanche of data for the pilot. The collision avoidance system constantly warned the pilot through cockpit lights and audio. However, because of the high speed at which racepods flew, the warnings were often ineffective, resulting in split-second incidents. The actual skill needed to pilot a racepod at speed in a pack was to be in control of that virtual safety bubble encapsulating the craft. If a pilot couldn't sustain that fine line guided by instrumentation feedback, they had to endure the consequences of safety being compromised. Autopilot did not exist in skyracing. Olivia's inertial measurement unit fed the Ghost Pod graphic display. The Ghost Pod visualisation system constantly updated Olivia's position, velocity, and attitude in real-time and compared her previous circuit position with her current and projected position to win. Electronic beacons mapped out the sky circuit boundary from side to side, top to bottom, via a projected display visible only from inside the cockpit. A narrow ravine or up to a maximum of 40 metres in open country could dictate the circuit width. They capped the ceiling altitude at 80 metres. Deviate outside those limits and audio alerts would automatically kick in and the Race Traffic Controller would be in the pilot's ear without delay.

Spectators worldwide had a selection of eight multi-viewer live feeds from SEN TV via the SkyRing cameras and live streams from the multitude of onboard cameras. The SkyRace GP app on PDs delivered all the vision plus race data, real-time tracking and Ghost Pod information for all racepods. This symbiotic connectivity solidified SkyRace GP as the number one live sporting event.

Communications between pilots and their Team Chief or engineer were private, to a point. Pilots used a dedicated radio channel to communicate with their Team Chief or engineer, but the SkyRace GP app or SEN TV could broadcast all conversations publicly. Teams also listened to the broadcasts to gain information, so some instructions between pilot and Team Chief were in code, such as Execute Fife or Tactic Tree to communicate strategy. Finding the right balance to convey accurate information without giving everything away was the key. Internal team radio communications remained private, meaning teams could strategise openly before talking to the pilot. One voice spoke to the pilot throughout the race to prevent confusion and minimise an overload of information from multiple voices talking simultaneously. The relationship continuity during the race remained familiar and consistent, especially when pilot emotions ran high when frustrated with an instruction they didn't agree with.

Aleeza and her father watched the race progress in the McRory Racing pit with the rest of the crew.

The rules permitted all teams two pit stops during the 420 kilometre race. Most pilots didn't use any, keeping them in reserve for an emergency. Pilots were competing against each other in the air, but ultimately they were racing the clock.

Having completed nine laps with one lap remaining, Olivia had moved into clear third position behind her teammate, Max Schroder. Her Ghost Pod display registered her current position was faster than her previous circuit time, but she needed to fly faster if she wanted to reach her projected position to win.

'Do not to overtake Schroder,' Gordie instructed Olivia.

'I'm faster, Gordie. You know that.'

'If you pass Max, Takata is on your tail and he might take both of you out.'

Olivia considered Gordie's instruction. 'I can't believe it,' Olivia finally snarled over the radio. 'You're trying to screw me, Gordie. I can't tell you how pissed off I am right now.'

'Copy that, Olivia. We'll chat afterwards.'

'We will.'

Schroder was doing his best to out manoeuvre her every move, to block Olivia from passing. Then, as they approached the western horn, the tricky hairpin bend, Olivia made the most of the three-dimensional space and climbed just above and to the left of Schroder. She paused. Abruptly, she flicked her joystick. Olivia barrel rolled over the top of him before descending, perfectly timed to come out of the bend in front, trapping Takata behind Schroder.

'Fuck,' Gordie exhaled in the pit. 'What the fuck was that?'

Aleeza whispered to her father, 'Olivia is doing, Olivia.'

'I wouldn't expect anything less. That move was audacious.'

Olivia pulled away from Schroder and crept up on Bianca Simmons, the #1 pilot for X Force, in first place. '*This is it*,' Olivia thought. '*I've got one chance to do this.*'

Olivia and Bianca turned into the home straight, literally stacked above one another, Olivia on the upper flight level. Both women pushed their machines to the max before Bianca's racepod shuddered.

'Look at her battery! It was in yellow, now it's in the red!' Sportscaster Katie Kang in the SEN commentary box screamed. 'Has the X Force racepod battery failed? Will she make it?'

At that moment, the X Force racepod died, forced into 'turtle' power mode served by the emergency supplementary battery. Bianca

Simmons slowed to 30km/h and descended, only the basic features available to make a safe landing. She did not finish.

In the McRory pit, Brad Hazzard threw Aleeza an apprehensive look as the crew cheered.

Olivia remained vigilant and throttled hard along the last three kilometres and took the chequered flag. Max Schroder kept Takata Jun confined and came in second.

After the race, an agitated Olivia stepped from her cockpit and marched into the McRory pit and confronted Aleeza. 'Was it your idea to get Max to block me?'

The accusation shocked Aleeza. 'I didn't ask anyone to block you, Olivia. Honest.'

Olivia walked over to the McRory Team Chief. 'Was it you, Gordie?'

'The team comes first, Olivia, but I–'

'Fuck you!'

Aleeza sidled up to Olivia. 'What are you going to do?' she asked.

Olivia didn't respond. Instead, she threw her helmet at Gordie and stormed off.

After the post-race scrutineering, the podium ceremony and media interviews were over, a crowd milled around the pilots. Brad Hazzard and Aleeza watched Olivia speaking with Henri Rossi and Zetta Minn from the Lazzrini team before Sergio Pirozzi joined them.

'What do you think she'll do?' Brad asked Aleeza.

'I have an uneasy feeling we've lost Olivia,' she expressed with a tinge of sadness in her voice as they considered her sister. 'Let's get a drink.'

'Before a race?'

'It's my mother's birthday and my sister isn't talking to me and she's about to,' she thought about her words, 'leave the team. I need a drink. Are you coming?'

A short time later, Brad, Aleeza and her father sat away from the McRory crew in Rohlf's Bar when the SkyRace GP Race Director, Perry Calver, appeared on the wall monitor. Chatter in the bar subsided to listen to the impromptu media conference.

'Thank you for joining me at such short notice,' Perry Calver began. 'There has been a formal request from the Lazzrini Race Team for a pilot swap in the Division 1 race tomorrow. The Lazzrini Race Team Principal, Sergio Pirozzi, has informed the Race Committee of the severity of Marco Franks injury. He will be recovering for the rest of the season. I repeat, Marco Franks will not return for the remainder of the 2048 race season. According to SkyRace GP rules, where an unanticipated injury or event preventing a pilot from competing in Division 1 occurs, the disadvantaged team can offer the winner of the Division 2 race at the current meet the opportunity to fly for them. The Lazzrini Race Team has formally offered Olivia Martin from McRory Racing, the winner of the Division 2 event today, the opportunity to swap teams and fly for the Lazzrini Race Team. Olivia Martin has accepted this offer and will replace the injured Marco Franks on the Lazzrini Race Team for tomorrow's Division 1 race.' Murmurs rippled throughout the small media contingent. 'Olivia Martin's existing race points in Division 2 will transfer to Division 1 pilot and team standings tomorrow. McRory Racing will keep the winning team points for the race today so they are not disadvantaged. McRory Racing will also receive Marco Franks' points transfer. Thank you.'

Sergio Pirozzi appeared on the screen. 'For any rookie pilot, a Division 1 Lazzrini Race Team seat is a long-held dream and Olivia Martin is no exception,' he explained. 'No one should stand in the way of Olivia realising her full potential.'

'The media is running hot after this swap shop announcement,' Harvie Stedman the SEN commentator reported, 'with some branding Olivia Martin a traitor, a defector, others, a maverick for swapping teams mid-season. What do you think her chances are in the race tomorrow against her sister, the current World Champion, Aleeza Martin?'

'It has been an ambition of Olivia's to fly in Division 1. Now Lazzrini will give her that opportunity. This is the first time siblings have flown against each other in a SkyRace GP. We will witness history. Two sisters, two pilots in excellent form, flying against each other, representing the top teams on points. What more could we ask for? Some events stick with us because they have significant meaning and value for us. Believe me, tomorrow will be one of those days.'

Nicolas Martin turned to his eldest daughter. 'How are you feeling?'

'I'd be lying if I told you I'm alright. I feel sick in my stomach.' Aleeza's PD buzzed. She read the text and responded at once. 'They wanted me for media. Not tonight.'

'I'll do it.' Brad sprang to his feet and was gone.

Gordie wandered over to Aleeza's table. 'Just so you know, I didn't tell Schroder to block Olivia,' he confessed. 'The decision to keep Olivia behind Max was to keep Takata from overtaking. It was best for the team. Second and third was a better option than Takata winning.'

'I know,' Aleeza acknowledged. 'Olivia knew that, but there was something else driving her.'

Nicolas' PD buzzed on the table. He picked it up and read the text. 'It's Olivia. She needs to talk.'

'Go, go,' Aleeza urged him. 'She needs her father tonight.'

As Nicolas got up to leave, Gordie touched his arm. 'Tell her there are no hard feelings, I understand, and that barrel roll stunt was fucking awesome flying.'

'I'm going for a wander,' Aleeza informed Gordie. 'Clear my head.'

Gordie smiled at his #1 pilot. 'Not too late. You need a good night's sleep.'

'I might find it hard to close my eyes tonight, Gordie. It's been an eventful day.'

Saturday night in the entertainment quarter was pulsating with crowds and activity. A live band played in the background as Aleeza strolled through the carnival rides, something she usually did with Olivia, but not tonight. Superfans recognised and congratulated her on becoming the world champ and wished her luck for tomorrow as they quickly posed for photos. Brad and his family emerged from the throng and approached her.

'How are you feeling about tomorrow?' Brad asked.

Before Aleeza responded, Klara blurted out, 'Olivia's a traitor!'

'Hey, enough of that type of language. Be polite,' Astrid scolded her daughter.

'Do you know what that word means, Klara?' Brad quizzed her.

'That's what they said on TV,' Klara submissively replied in her defence. 'A traitor flies a plane, but now Olivia isn't flying a McRory plane.'

'That's an aviator, you idiot,' Amalia scoffed at her sister.

'Olivia is following her dreams,' Aleeza told the little girls. 'Tomorrow will be a tough day for all of us,' she directed at Brad.

'That it will,' he agreed. 'Okay, bedtime for you two. See you tomorrow.' With that, the family moved on.

Further along, Lukas de Castro and his entourage of women sat at an outside café table, garnering as much attention as he could from fans wanting to get a photo with the flashy pilot.

Lukas spotted Aleeza. 'Hey, Martin #1! Martin #2 has betrayed McRory and deserted.' His gang laughed at his comment. 'I'm going to whip both your arses tomorrow.'

Aleeza didn't stop walking and didn't react to his verbal swipe. She spied the Dream Immersion pods lined up and decided to have a go. A distraction was what she needed.

At the same time in the Lazzrini hangar, Olivia and the Lazzrini crew had just finished customising her racepod cockpit for the upcoming race. Henri Rossi and Olivia shared a moment.

'I have to admit,' Henri started, 'your race strategy today was flawless. The barrel roll was inspired.'

'Thanks. So, you feel I'm ready for D1 now?' she questioned sarcastically.

Henri smiled. 'You picked up everything we ran through tonight with ease. I am impressed. It was an accelerated learning curve.'

An extended gaze between the pair exposed an awkward moment of attraction as pupils dilated.

'Anyway, I'm damn tired and I need to sleep,' Olivia stated, breaking the connection.

'Yes, me as well.'

Henri observed Olivia as she left the hangar. *'Don't do it,'* he told himself. *'Don't go back there.'* Henri vowed never to pursue a female pilot after the death of his then girlfriend Connie Moretti in the French SkyRace GP five years ago, and he had no plans to break that rule. *'This is a test.'*

Zetta Minn entered the hangar. 'How did she go?'

Henri didn't answer at first, still in his head, convincing himself to keep his promise. 'Ehm, good, sì, very good. She... she definitely has una scintilla, a spark.'

'You've changed your tune,' Zetta admitted with a sly grin.

Henri caught her expression. 'I'm going to push her tomorrow, to her limits, to see if she has what it takes to fly D1.'

Chapter Three

SkyRace GP Division 1 Pilot Standings coming into the USA event.

Position	# Pilot	Team	Points	Chile	Argentina	Australia	Nigeria	India	Madagascar
1	Aleeza Martin (#1)	McRory	109	20	25	14	20 (+1)	4	25
2	Lukas de Castro (#1)	Eagle One	98	14	22	13	11	18	20
3	Marco Franks (#1)	Lazzrini	83	12	13	20 (+1)	25	13	DNF
4	Jing Zhao (#1)	XPang-Fu	82	18	5	22	3	20	14
5	Zetta Minn (#2)	Lazzrini	78	13 (+1)	18	4	5	25	11
6	Paul van der Meer (#1)	Vogel Machina	72	25	20	12	13	DNF	2
7	Royce Simms (#1)	AeroWing	69	11	11	3	18	22	4
8	Aimee Walton-Dewa (#1)	Red Roo	66	22	12	25	4	DNF	3
9	Brad Hazzard (#2)	McRory	64	5	14 (+1)	5	12	14	13
10	Matilda Vettel (#1)	X Force	62	2	4	11	22	11	12
11	Tamas Hutlassa (#1)	Schneider	55	3	DNF	2	14	12 (+1)	22 (+1)
12	Morgan Patel (#2)	AeroWing	25	DNF	3	18	2	2	
13	Seo Hye-bin (#1)	Watson-Cruz	21	4		DNF		3	18
14	Rita Perez (#1)	Foxx	7		2		DNF	5	DNF
15	Kawano Takayuki (#1)	Hoverflyers	5		DNF		DNF		5

SkyRace GP scoring system per event

Position	1st	2nd	3rd	4th	5th	6th	7th	8th	9th	10th	11th	12th		Fastest Event Lap
Points	25	22	20	18	14	13	12	11	5	4	3	2		1

'Cleared for 15 minutes, Aleeza,' Dylan called out.

'Good to go,' Aleeza acknowledged as she continued her limber-up routine for the sprint qualifying session.

'Lukas has just clocked the third fastest,' Gordie informed Aleeza. '14:23'.

'And Olivia?'

'Pushes her back to sixth fastest on 14:35. Zetta Minn is next up on grid.'

'Who's on poll besides Lukas?' Aleeza asked.

'Aimee Walton-Dewa from Red Roo clocked 14:18 and Paul van der Meer for Vogel Machina clocked 14.21; Gordie read from his tablet screen.

'Where's Brad?'

'Third row in ninth. He flew 14:41.'

Aleeza was last in the sprint qualifying session. Being the World Champion had its perks, like going last to see what time she had to beat to make poll position.

They finalised grid positions after thirty minutes, and Zetta Minn and Aleeza snatched poll position with 14:14 and 14:20 respectively, with Aimee Walton-Dewa. This pushed everyone back. The coming hour would see race officials complete pre-race pilot weigh-ins and random racepod scrutineering.

The worldwide media frenzy hit fever pitch as it set the stage for the Martin sisters historic battle in the sky. Online stories titled, "The Martins are Coming!", "My Favourite Martin" and "The Day the Earth Stood Still" were capitalising and speculating on which of the Martin sisters would win the first sibling contest in SkyRace GP history. The worldwide audience exploded as social media spread the word, whipping the story into hysteria, and now the world eagerly anticipated the extraordinary event.

The post qualifying, pre-race media conference was more frantic than usual as more media reps packed the conference room. On the small stage sat the top three qualifying pilots, comfortably seated in big lounge chairs and using head microphones.

'Quiet please,' the MC insisted, standing off to the right of the small stage. 'Welcome everyone to the United States SkyRace GP Division 1 pilots' pre-race media conference. Due to the high number of attendees this morning, we're running a little behind schedule, so we'll have to limit the number of questions. I'd like to introduce our SkyRacing pilots, Aleeza Martin from McRory Racing, Aimee Walton-Dewa from Red Roo Racing and Zetta Minn from the Lazzrini Race Team. Welcome to the three of you. Our first question is from Gina Haggerty from Unlimited Sports.'

The reporter stood, and they handed a microphone to her. 'Good morning, my question is for Aleeza Martin. How are you feeling competing against your sister for the first time and do you think you'll beat her?'

'I'm feeling a little more apprehensive about going into this race, I must admit, but this race is no different from other races because I'm out there to do my best for McRory Racing.'

'Do you think you'll beat Olivia?' the reporter repeated.

Aleeza smiled. 'I don't know. Stick around and we'll both find out.'

'Next question is from Nathan Sepro from E-Motion Ezine.'

'My question is for Zetta Minn. How does it feel having a new pilot in the Lazzrini team and how do you think Olivia Martin will go today?'

'It's sad that Marco isn't with us today, but I think Olivia is an extremely capable replacement. Olivia proved that yesterday. Who does a barrel roll like that? No one except Olivia! It helps to be a little crazy to fly at these speeds, adrenaline mixed with fear. Olivia and I will push our racepods to their limits and go all out to make sure the Lazzrini team finishes in the top three.'

'Next question is from Jimena D'Amico, from Murdoch Sports.'

Jimena took the microphone 'Hello. My question is for Aimee Watson-Dewa. Aimee, are you surprised Lukas de Castro is not up there with you?'

'Who?' All the newshounds laughed.

'Lukas de—' the reporter awkwardly began.

'Just yanking your chain, Jimena. No, Lukas is a show pony and an average pilot at best. I think all of us here know that. These two pilots beside me are the real deal and the pilots to beat.'

In the Lazzrini hangar, Olivia had one eye on the media conference screen and the other on a tablet device reading through all the D1 pilot qualifying times.

'If you can fly like you did yesterday, I'm sure you'll beat Aleeza,' Henri assured her. 'You know her strengths and weaknesses.'

Olivia was feeling more comfortable around Henri. 'As she does mine. These are different racepods, but yeah, I think I've got a good feel for the extra power.'

'Our strategy is simple. Stay with the front pack, and when the time is right, we'll make our move. I'll give you the radio codes.'

'Tree-Tree-Zulu for defensive blocking and Niner-Fife-Bravo to fly aggressively.'

'Correct. Remember, Olivia, no risk, no glory.'

'No risk, no glory,' she repeated.

An alert sounded over the event speakers in the hangar. 'Start grid walk through will begin in five minutes,' the announcer confirmed.

'Time to meet and greet for the second time this weekend,' Olivia said as she picked up her helmet. 'It feels strange doing this twice in one weekend.'

The start grid felt even more chaotic than usual for Olivia. She was the centre of attention compared to those pilots around her. Race officials had to intervene to manage the unexpected fan queue to have pictures taken with her. Brad's wife, Astrid, shuffled Klara and Amalia onto the line to meet Olivia. Olivia watched out the corner of her eye as the two girls refused to stay put and clearly resisted their mother's instructions until Astrid gave up and all three left the queue and walked away. Disappointed, Olivia maintained a professional appearance. She bit her lip and kept her composure, not wanting to express emotions in her very public workplace before a race. She took a deep breath and focused on the task at hand.

Regrettably, Aleeza witnessed the children's reaction from her vantage point on the start grid as Nicolas Martin approached and gave her a hug, and wished her luck. They both looked across at the pack surrounding Olivia. 'Always the party girl. How was she last night?'

'Guarded is the word I would use to describe her state of mind last night,' her father honestly replied. 'She knows I'm the connection between the two of you at the moment until the dust settles.'

'It's a damn big move.'

'It sure is. But Olivia has always been someone who can go it alone and ends up landing on her feet. You are methodical. Olivia seems to be at home in chaos.'

'True. It feels strange that she's on the other side now. She is someone I have to beat at all costs. That's fresh territory.'

'Up there,' he pointed, 'not down here. I'd better go and wish her luck.'

'So, who are you going for?' Aleeza teased.

'You know better than that.' Nicolas walked away, then turned around. 'You know Olivia has always been my favourite.' He blew her a kiss and smiled.

'How are the nerves?' Gordie asked, walking up beside Aleeza.

'So-so.'

'You know what I'm going to say.'

'Yes, get comfortable being uncomfortable.'

'Don't treat this race any differently.'

'But it is, Gordie. It's personal. I'm racing my sister.'

'You are the D1 World Champion, and this is her first Division 1 race. I think you have the edge. Be professional and don't let emotion get in the way.'

'Of course.'

'And remember, Olivia is Oz over the radio.'

'Here we are, only seconds away from the most anticipated start of a SkyRace GP race in its history,' Harvie Stedman, the SEN sportscaster, enthused over vision of racepods hovering in their tiered grid positions patiently awaiting the start. 'This adrenaline-fueled competition brings together the most skilled pilots and technologically advanced racepods on the planet, ready to push their limits and exceed all expectations. The United States SkyRace GP event has raised the excitement level a couple of notches for tens of millions of fans eagerly waiting to see their favourite pilots and racepods from around the world. Aleeza Martin, the World Champion, is taking on her sister, Olivia Martin, in her first ever Division 1 race. This is the first time siblings have gone head to head in a Division 1 race. Extraordinary circumstances got us to this point and I'm sure more extraordinary action will unfold throughout the race today. Here we go, countdown lights on...lights out! And they're off!'

The unique sound of SkyRace GP Division 1 racepods was a visceral and intense experience. They had the enhanced power of the ducted air intake bladeless thruster embedded at the rear of the airframe, which gave them a distinct hum, like a jet engine spinning up but at a far more tolerable level. The speed was breathtaking, the precision of the pilots awe-inspiring. The race was a test of skill, endurance, and strategy, with every decision made in the heat of the moment having the potential to make or break both pilots' and team's chances.

Polesitter Zetta Minn got away cleanly to take the lead into the first corner, followed closely by the other two polesitters, Aleeza Martin, then Aimee Walton-Dewa. Live feeds from the SkyRing cameras, pilot helmets, racepod cockpits and racepod fuselages were vision switched by SEN technicians to accompany their sports commentary team.

Olivia's heart thumped so hard in her chest she could hear it. Henri told her to be cautious and maintain her position through the zigzag section immediately following the start. If she could sustain that position through the first lap, her nerves would settle and her flying intuition would kick in, creating opportunities to advance as the field opened up. He was right. After the first four laps Olivia had advanced three places to fifth position.

Aleeza maintained her second position from the start, as did Zetta in first and Aimee in third.

'Oz is fife,' Gordie reported to Aleeza over the radio. 'Loco is fow-er.'

'Copy that.' Aleeza expected Olivia and Lukas to keep advancing when given the chance. Her Ghost Pod present position had improved by a couple of seconds over her previous position, so Aleeza needed to maintain that competitive edge. 'And Brad?'

'Wrong side of the dozen,' Gordie responded.

At the midpoint of the race, only two teams had lost racepods. AeroWing's #2 pilot Morgan Patel withdrew due to a power issue and Hoverflyers #1 pilot Kawano Takayuki retired with faulty navigation equipment.

As the kilometres ticked by, the tension mounted and the excitement was building towards a crescendo. The fastest five had made no pit stops and were in the final stage of the race as they zoomed past the grandstand to begin their last lap. Two more teams abandoned the race because of a mid-air collision that damaged rotor housings and blades, reducing the field to 20 teams.

'The flock of five are keeping such tight formation it might be difficult for Olivia Martin to make a move this close to home,' Harvie Stedman the sportscaster suggested. 'Wait! Lukas de Castro has cut under Aimee Walton-Dewa on the first hairpin bend of the zigzag section and has moved into third! Incredible flying from the Brazilian champion. He said this was his race in earlier interviews and he could be right. Now heading towards the open plain in the southeastern circuit, there is a bit of jostling going on as the sky circuit widens to 40 metres and the first sweeping right-hand curve.'

'Niner-Fife-Bravo,' Henri conveyed to Olivia.

'Roger that.'

'Gosh! Look at Olivia Martin! She has hammered it and also overtaken the Red Roo #1 pilot Aimee Walton-Dewa. I tell you what, Olivia Martin is not fearful when it comes to using that extra power at her disposal. Olivia is now gaining on Lukas de Castro! This is amazing. Olivia Martin, the rookie from Lazzrini Race Team, has pitched her nose-down and passed Lukas de Castro, clocking the fastest speed of 256 kilometres per hour and securing the third position. Wow! She is poking the edges of the flight envelope, testing the limits of her D1 racepod. Olivia is now behind her sister, Aleeza Martin, and is closing in. This is phenomenal flying by the Division 1 newbie.'

'Oz is on your tail,' Gordie told Aleeza. 'Loco is on hers.'

'Copy that.'

The southwestern circuit tracked close to the sheer cliff faces with random overhanging rocky outcrops. Of the five racepods, Zetta Minn flew closest to the escarpment. Without warning, a flock of startled Cliff Swallows took flight from their cliff hollows and struck Zetta's racepod. The other racepods rolled away from the collision zone, saving themselves from being impacted by birds.

Dozens of birds clogged and choked Zetta's rotor blades and housings, causing total power failure and loss of control.

'Where did they come from?' Harvie Stedman exclaimed to his audience. 'I thought the cliffs were empty. The swallows migrated south last month? It's a day of firsts.'

'Mayday! Mayday!' Zetta screamed. 'I've lost control.' Her racepod smashed sideways into an overhanging ledge at 240km/h, glanced off into the cliff face before gravity took over and it plummeted straight down, crashing and rolling. It came to rest right side up under the ledge.

'Accident alert, accident alert, rescue vehicle en route,' the Race Traffic Controller warned pilots.

'I'm okay,' Zetta announced groggily over the radio as her airbags deflated. Zetta popped the transparent cockpit canopy and waved, knowing the cameras would be on her. She could see the rescue quadcopter approaching. She removed her helmet and hurled it out of the cockpit, frustrated her race was over. The massive ledge she hit lurched and groaned. Unmistakable cracking, rumbling and crumbling compelled Zetta to look up. The enormous ledge fell, crushing her.

The SEN broadcast technical director, on seven second broadcast delay, managed to vision switch their live feed away from the fate of Zetta Minn before the tens of millions watching knew what had happened. The last images broadcast of Zetta were of her waving to her audience.

Viewers were back in the cockpit with Aleeza Martin, now in the lead. Olivia crept closer, as did Lukas, as the pack of four entered the rhino horn hairpin bend on the furthest western point of the circuit.

Olivia knew this section of the course intimidated Aleeza, and she was going to capitalise on that. She flew under Aleeza, Lukas flew above Aleeza, sandwiching the World Champion. In a tight, stacked vertical formation, the hairpin approached. They all had to throttle down to make the turn.

The cliff wall was reminiscent of the Vikos Gorge in Greece for Aleeza. That crash sensation flashed to mind for a fleeting moment, causing Aleeza to balk, and Olivia pounced. She exploited a split second and planted her foot on the right pedal to engage right yaw axis and pivoted around the corner, then immediately pushed her throttle to accelerate out of the turn. Lukas took a wider arc but still came out ahead of Aleeza, who had slipped back to third.

'To everyone watching this masterclass in SkyRacing by Olivia Martin, you are witnessing history,' Katie Kang gushed. 'I've got goosebumps! The hairs on my arms have stood to attention. I don't think I have ever seen a stamp of dominance like this from a rookie in their first race in all my years of broadcasting the SkyRace GP.'

Aleeza was not spent yet. She gained on Lukas and levelled above him along the second stretch of cliffs in the northwestern section. Aleeza maintained her position with Lukas as both pilots edged closer to Olivia.

'Go Aleeza!' Gordie yelled at the monitor in the pit as Dylan and the rest of the crew cheered her on.

Into the second last straight, like a phoenix rising from the ashes, Aleeza, a symbol of resilience and strength for McRory Racing, reined in her sister.

'Both Alpha and Lima approaching,' Henri warned Olivia. 'Tree-Tree-Zulu.'

'Roger that.' Olivia knew the slightest mistake could mean the difference between victory and defeat. She switched her rear-view camera to one of her displays. Olivia navigated with precision along the projected fastest route, rolling and pitching at just the right moment to block Aleeza and then Lukas, while flying at maximum speed.

As the final tight bend approached, the gap between the three racepods narrowed, and the pressure intensified for Olivia, as she could not fend off both veteran pilots. The determined pilots remained focused and alert, trying to anticipate their opponent's movements, and seized every opportunity to gain an advantage. As they rounded the bend, Olivia was only marginally in front.

'Here they go into the final straight and at the moment it could be any of these three teams claiming victory,' Harvie Stedman speculated. 'Lazzrini, McRory or Eagle One. The entire grandstand is on their feet cheering! It's Olivia Martin still in front, but here comes the World Champion Aleeza Martin! Not to be outdone, Lukas de Castro is coming in over the top of the two sisters! This would have to be one of the closest finishes since the German SkyRace GP in '46 when we had half a second separating first and third. With two kilometres left, they are neck and neck after flying 420 kilometres. It looks like de Castro is just leading. No, Aleeza Martin's front wing has nudged in front.

Olivia was determined. Henri's words came to mind: *no risk, no glory*. She forced her throttle as far as it would go and hoped for the best.

'It's Aleeza Martin still in front, but here comes her younger sister!' Harvie Stedman yelled. 'Wow! I honestly can't tell you which pilot has won. It's that close. They have shut the official timing board down while race officials confirm the times and places. The ChronoLaser system tracks the racepods' transponders down to the millisecond, so that's what race officials will be checking. There it is! Olivia Martin has won in a time of 2 hours, 7 minutes, 5 seconds and 500 milliseconds! Lukas de Castro was in second place with 2 hours, 7 minutes, 5 seconds and 620 milliseconds. Amazing! Aleeza Martin came in third at 2 hours, 7 minutes, 5 seconds and 870 milliseconds! This was closer than Germany in '46! Just 0.37 of a second between first and third! What a phenomenal finish to this extraordinary race! Let's have a look at that finish in ultra slow-mo from a few angles.'

'You won!' Henri bellowed over the radio.

'Did I? Has it been confirmed?' Olivia asked in disbelief.

'We have confirmation of the times. It's official. Aleeza was third. You won D1!'

Once the winner had crossed the line, as each racepod crossed the line behind them, their race was finished, regardless of their position or what lap they were on. All racepods then landed in the closed start grid for post-race pilot weigh-ins and scrutineering of racepods.

Subdued scenes followed as a noticeably distressed Olivia spoke with Sergio Pirozzi and Henri Rossi about Zetta Minn. It seemed a bittersweet moment for Olivia and the entire Lazzrini team. Word was filtering through the teams and spectators about the unusual nature of the accident. Many were in shock.

'I'm so sorry to hear about Zetta,' Aleeza commiserated with Olivia as they hugged. 'I loved Zetta. She was a rare breed among pilots. A genuine friend.' They both wiped away tears as they parted.

'She was,' Olivia agreed. 'What a fucking crazy thing to happen!'

'Yep. No one could see that coming. No one.' A hard silence lingered. 'Congratulations,' Aleeza said as she touched Olivia's arm. 'You knocked me off my perch.' She hugged her sister again and whispered, 'this time.' Olivia sobbed.

A small crowd surrounded the pair with PDs in hand, filming and photographing the moment, as did the single SEN media drone broadcasting to the world.

As they separated, Nicolas Martin approached his daughters wearing an uneasy smile. 'Stressful day at the office.'

Olivia burst out crying when she saw him. 'Dad!' She embraced her father as if her life depended upon it.

SkyRace GP Division 1 Pilot Standings after the USA event. Yellow indicates leader.

Location	Olivia	total	Aleeza	total	Lukas	total
USA	25 (1st)	119	20 (3rd)	129	22 (2nd)	120

'It is with deep sadness that I must pass on some distressing news about one of our much admired pilots,' SkyRace GP Race Director, Perry Calver, conveyed to the waiting crowd and broadcast audience. 'The Lazzrini Race Team Principal, Sergio Pirozzi, advised the Race Committee, emergency doctors at The Hospitals of Providence in El Paso have confirmed the death of pilot Zetta Minn, the #1 pilot in Division 1 from the Lazzrini Race Team, due to injuries sustained in a freak accident towards the end of the race. Our hearts and condolences go out to her family and friends, many of whom are here today. I have launched an official investigation into the accident. Vale Zetta Minn.'

After a sombre podium ceremony, Aleeza declined all media interviews. As the winner, Olivia had a contractual obligation to give at least one interview. Olivia granted Harvie Stedman the sportscaster from SEN that interview.

'Thanks for talking with me at a difficult time, and my condolences. Zetta Minn was one of the most charismatic and skilful pilots SkyRace GP has seen and we will truly miss her in the competition.' He paused to change tack. 'A SkyRace GP is a spectacle like no other, a thrilling display of speed, skill, and daring that leaves everyone breathless and wanting more. Today was a first for siblings competing against each other. You won your debut Division 1 race, becoming the first rookie to do so. How does that make you feel?'

Olivia wiped her face of remnant tears before she spoke. 'Honestly, Harvie, I feel numb. I'm stunned. Zetta was a friend, a colleague, and a fierce competitor in the air. I feel for her daughter, Andrea, who lives with disability. That little girl will grow up without a mother, and I can relate to that. I was a little older, but life without a mother is difficult for any child.' She wiped a tear away. 'As for the firsts, this is the first SkyRace I have taken part in where a colleague lost their life. That will stay with me forever. As for the other firsts, I haven't really processed any of it. I'm sure I will in the coming days. Thank you.' Olivia turned and walked away from the microphone as Lukas de Castro hovered, looking at Harvie, waiting to be asked some questions.

'Back to you, Katie,' Harvie insisted.

Roselyn Nash, #2 pilot in Division 2 for Lazzrini, approached Olivia. 'Got a minute? I want to show you something.' Olivia followed Roselyn away from the crowds to a quieter location. Roselyn pulled out her PD. 'I got this from one of our crew. Listen.' She played a video that pointed to nothing in particular but inadvertently recorded a conversation behind the camera.

'That's Brad Hazzard's voice,' Olivia uttered.

'Brad telling Max Schroder, Nino Lombardi and me to block you at all costs in yesterday's race.' Roselyn played it twice.

'Why are you showing me this now?'

Roselyn began to cry. 'Zetta was like a sister to me; we hung out together off circuit. I'm flying out in an hour to Naples, to help Natasha with Andrea. Natasha's devastated. She doesn't know how to tell Andrea. We'll explain to Andrea what happened when I get there. Anyway, I just wanted you to know that you made the right decision to swap teams mid-season. Zetta made that happen. She saw your potential. She would be so proud.'

Olivia took Roselyn's hands in hers. 'Thank you, Roselyn. If you need anything for Andrea, money for carers or her education, anything, let me know. I want to help.'

'I will. Sergio said the Lazzrini Race Team will setup a trust for Andrea.'

'Good. Are you okay?'

'Yes, yes. I have to go; I'll be late for my flight.'

'Of course, go. Oh, and for what it's worth, I'll be pitching for you to replace Zetta in D1, not Nino. I think you're the better pilot.'

'Thank you.'

'And send that video to me.' Olivia headed away from the crowd; she needed time to process everything that had happened. When she reached the Lazzrini hangar, she discovered Henri sitting in a corner by himself with a beer in his hand.

'The second death for our team in five years,' Henri said softly. 'We lost Connie in France in '43.'

'I remember that. I remember reading about the circumstances. Very sad,' Olivia sympathised. 'I'm sorry you're going through this again, Henri.' She remembered the importance of empathy and emotional support in the workplace from her air ambulance days.

'Maybe in our strange world, this very public world we live in, emotions play a larger role in communication and bonding,' Henri postulated. 'Perhaps this will bring us, you and I, closer, to build a better team. Emotional responses can demonstrate our passion for work without being destructive. Sorry, I am rambling.'

'No, no, it's important to express our thoughts and feelings during times of grief. Got a spare one of those?' She pointed to his beer.

'Where are my manners? Sorry.' He reached into the bar fridge beside him, then handed her a beer. 'To Zetta,' he toasted, raising his bottle.

'To Zetta.' Olivia met him with a chink of glass.

They both drank. The silence between them was neither difficult nor awkward, but necessary.

Aleeza wandered back to her accommodation. As she sat alone in her dome after the traumatic day, she couldn't help but feel the weight of loneliness settling upon her. This feeling was all too familiar to Aleeza. She poured her energy into her job with no one to share in her successes or listen to her struggles. However, she knew she wasn't alone in experiencing this emotion.

Chapter Four

Aleeza and Olivia were not speaking to one another. The two sisters, the two McRory Racing teammates for the first half of the 2048 season, were now in a hostile relationship. The once vibrant and inseparable sisters and friends had found themselves in a rift, their bond fractured. Days turned into weeks as the two young women remained distant. They no longer called or texted each other.

Their father had tried to intervene, hoping to bridge the gap and mend their broken relationship. However, his efforts were met with resistance. Olivia was determined to remain stubborn, refusing to address the underlying issues that had caused their falling out.

The reasons behind their hostility remained a mystery to most. Speculation and rumours circulated; the media formed their own narrative to explain the sudden disintegration of their friendship. But the truth was known to Aleeza and Olivia, and a few within their inner circles. A media stunt followed by a private spat during the Spanish SkyRace GP had triggered the bitterness. Aleeza said things to Olivia she regretted as soon as the words left her mouth.

SkyRace GP Division 1 Pilot Standings after the Spanish event. Yellow indicates leader.

Location	Olivia	total	Aleeza	total	Lukas	total
USA	25 (1st)	119	20 (3rd)	129	22 (2nd)	120
Spain	14 (5th)	133	11 (8th)	140	25 (1st)	145

Olivia failed to arrive early to the Japanese race weekend and her dome accommodation remained empty. Nobody saw her eating at Barney's or enjoying the entertainment quarter. The solemn scene struck those who knew them. Their typical merriment and friendly banter were absent. Their shared memories and inside jokes were now distant echoes. They also noticed an eerie stillness and obvious unease whenever Olivia and Aleeza encountered each other. They avoided eye contact, not even a curt nod when forced to acknowledge each other's presence.

The mood from the stage in the Japanese SkyRace GP pre-race media conference radiated tension. Lukas de Castro sat between Aleeza and Olivia in comfy leather lounge chairs, waiting in silence for media reporters from around the globe to finish taking their seats. The friction between Aleeza and Olivia was palpable. Team publicists and minders from all three teams stood to one side, ready to watch the interview.

'Welcome, everyone, to the Japanese SkyRace GP Division 1 pilots pre-race media conference,' the MC began. 'I'd like to introduce our fastest qualifiers, Aleeza Martin from McRory Racing, Lukas de Castro from Eagle One Racing and Olivia Martin from the Lazzrini Race Team. Welcome to the three of you. Let's start with a question to you first, Lukas. You won for the first time this season a couple of weeks ago in Spain, putting you at the top of the pilot's standings. Do you think you'll be back on the winner's podium by the end of today?'

'Well, it's not unknown territory for me, as you know. I've been in this position frequently over the four years I've been flying Division 1 for Eagle One Racing. After last year, many of you in this room wrote me off for this current season, but here I am,' he deliberately looked left then right, 'the meat in a Martin sandwich.' The room erupted into laughter while the sisters remained straight-faced.

'We'll take a question from Gemison Campos from GP Today,' the MC introduced.

A microphone was handed to the reporter as he stood. 'Thank you. Question for Lukas de Castro. Given you are 35 at the end of this year, middle-aged some would say, is retirement something you are thinking about?' Giggles peppered the room.

'Well, Gemison, as a fellow countryman, you were one of those who was less than sympathetic at the end of last season about my chances for this season. There are younger pilots, but I seem to get better with age, don't you think? No, I don't think about retirement.'

'Next question is from Naomi Shikichi from Rocket TV.'

Naomi took the microphone. 'Thank you. My question is for Olivia Martin. Many in the media have branded you a maverick for moving from McRory to Lazzrini mid-season. How does that label sit with you? Do you think it's a fair call?'

Olivia squirmed in her seat, still not comfortable in the full glare of the media spotlight. 'Well...well my understanding of a maverick is an unorthodox person, an independent-minded individual. I think that pretty much sums up my entire life. I'll wear that crown.'

'Next question is from Daniel Masolin from InSports Media.'

'Good morning. My question is for Aleeza Martin. You and your sister are like chalk and cheese when it comes to race preparation. Your training leading up to race weekends is highly disciplined, while Olivia reportedly indulges in pre-race partying. Given that Olivia won in Texas and placed fifth in Spain ahead of you, will you be considering a change to your training approach leading up to a race?'

Aleeza looked daggers at the reporter as murmurs ricocheted around the room. 'Danny, you know me. Short answer, no.'

A smirk rippled across Olivia's face.

'Just a follow-up question for Aleeza,' Daniel Masolin continued. 'We've had a couple of weeks to digest the recording your sister publicly released before the Spanish GP regarding your teammate Brad Hazzard instructing pilots to block her in the US Division 2 race. Do you think it was a wise move to release the recording publicly like that instead of handing it to the SkyRace GP Race Committee to deal with?'

The room fell silent in anticipation of her reaction. Aleeza thought about her answer before she responded. 'Some of you in the media have labelled Olivia a maverick. She is unorthodox, she does as she pleases, she always has, but this publicity stunt was totally irresponsible. Rather than go through the correct channels, she made Brad a target for vitriolic attacks and abuse in the public arena. People have tormented and ridiculed Brad and his family for the past weeks. I have said this privately to Olivia. The stunt was irresponsible, naïve, and callous. She should be ashamed of herself.'

Aleeza's comment was the detonation point for the room to explode with questions fired at both Olivia and Aleeza from reporters standing and yelling.

'That's it!' the MC shouted over the chorus of voices. 'This media conference is now over.'

McRory's publicist and minders briskly escorted Aleeza out of the room, carefully avoiding Olivia's vocal mockery just a few metres away.

Shallow water was the unique terrain of the Japanese SkyRace GP, setting it apart from other skyracing circuits. The sky circuit was above Lake Biwa, the largest freshwater lake on Honshu. Long pontoons with floating grandstands on either side formed the start/finish grid. The sky circuit went under the Biwako Bridge on one side and over the bridge on the return. Organisers rented several large tracts of disused agricultural land to set-up the entertainment quarter and camping grounds for FIFO spectators. SEN cameras were broadcasting from the six SkyRing airships in position with their VIP guests aboard.

Aleeza was preparing herself for the main event when Jericho Starling and a guest entered the McRory hangar. Jericho introduced him to Gordie and Brad, and eventually, they made a beeline to Aleeza.

'Aleeza, I would like you to meet Bayden Turner, Global Operations Manager for the Unicus Corporation, our newest sponsor.'

'Pleased to meet you, Aleeza. I'm a massive fan.' He extended his hand.

'Thank you.' She shook his hand firmly. 'Welcome aboard, Bayden. Tell me, what does the Unicus Corporation do?'

'We operate a suite of brands in fashion, cosmetics, fashion accessories and jewellery, perfumes, home decor, wines and spirits, and resorts,' he rattled off.

'That's a mouthful. I bet you've had to rehearse that pitch.'

'I have,' he smiled, 'and more than once. We're a multinational with a focus on luxury products.'

'Bayden was telling me Unicus has revenue of about 80 billion a year,' Jericho stated, to impress. 'Bayden has an idea he would like to run by you after the race. An endorsement proposal for you.'

'Give me a hint,' Aleeza fished with a grin.

Bayden, a charismatic, confident man barely in his 40s with peppered stubble, gladly took the bait. 'Unicus are about to launch an upmarket chain of stores around a lifestyle activewear brand called Empulsion. We'd like you to be the face of that brand. We feel you would be the perfect fit.'

'Aleeza cleared for 15 minutes. Good to go?' Dylan quietly interrupted.

'Good to go. Well, Bayden, nice to meet you, but I have to go to work,' she quipped. 'I trust I will see you after the race.'

'Yes, after the race. Good luck.'

Aleeza pointed to her left wrist. 'Always wear my monkey bracelet for luck. My mother gave it to me on my 13th birthday.' Six outstretched monkeys holding the foot of the next made up the chunky silver bracelet.

'The Japanese SkyRace GP atmosphere is electric,' began SEN sportscaster Katie Kang, as the broadcast showed the racepods in their tiered start grid formation. 'The weather on Lake Biwa is fantastic, a beautiful sunny day with a very light northwesterly breeze. Spectators have lined the lake's edge, and the much sought after floating grandstands have been sold out for months. As usual, the city council has closed the Biwako Bridge to traffic during the race and allowed spectators to fill it. Restrictions on watercraft and aircraft in the area, except for rescue craft, are also in place for the event. Not long now. Here we go, countdown lights on...lights out! And there they go! The swarm awakens! Lukas de Castro has started the adrenaline-fueled battle from the get-go, hovering out in front of the other polesitters, the Martin sisters.'

'The Eagle One racepod got a blistering jump on the Martin sisters,' Harvie Stedman agreed. 'The new single cell mass density battery racepods are using this season give lighter racepods a slight advantage with an extra boost from a standing start because of the power to weight ratio of their racepods.'

'So even a few kilos lighter is proving to be an advantage, Harvie. On socials, people continue to both roast and applaud Olivia Martin. Thousands of memes are reigniting the explosive story of McRory Racing pilot Brad Hazzard instructing other pilots to block Olivia Martin, his own teammate in Texas, a month ago. Since Olivia Martin released the hot mic audio recording the day before the Spanish SkyRace GP, it has gone hyperviral and has been trending ever since, as fans have their say. It continues to reverberate here at the Japanese GP.'

'Yes, Katie, there were some very vocal fans on both sides of the pits in Spain, and this story isn't disappearing anytime soon. There's unconfirmed chatter they might not offer Brad Hazzard a contract with McRory next season.'

The SkyRacing GP competition was one of the most physically and mentally demanding sports in the world. During a race, the pilot must maintain an exceptional level of focus and concentration, more so than road-based motorsports. Why? The third dimension. According to the research paper, Psychological Profile of Sports Performance published by Deakin University in 2047, concentration and attentional focus were important factors that influence an athlete's performance in a sport. Their study compared experienced SkyRace GP pilots with FE and Indy 500 drivers and found that skyracers developed quicker response times, better anticipation and mental parameters because of experience-specific adaptations to the third dimension requirements of flying. This adaptation of skyracing led to a higher level of attentiveness and concentration during the race. During training at the SkyRace Pilot Academy, blinking training had been a key focus for pilots, as the timing of blinking can increase or decrease the pilot's position in a race. A single blink at the wrong point in the sky circuit could lose a pilot as much as 20 metres and could lose as much as 500 metres worth of visual information per minute because of blinking. The adage of blink and you miss it definitely rang true for SkyRace GP pilots.

After 420 kilometres of fierce competition, Aleeza Martin stayed with the pack to secure second place behind Paul van der Meer, the #1 pilot at Vogel Machina. Olivia Martin finished outside a podium finish in fourth and Lukas de Castro finished back in seventh. It elevated Aleeza to the top of the Division 1 pilot standings yet again.

SkyRace GP Division 1 Pilot Standings after the Japanese event. Yellow indicates leader.

Location	Olivia	total	Aleeza	total	Lukas	total
USA	25 (1st)	119	20 (3rd)	129	22 (2nd)	120
Spain	14 (5th)	133	11 (8th)	140	25 (1st)	145
Japan	18 (4th)	151	22 (2nd)	162	12 (7th)	157

At the end of the race, superfans wanting autographs and photos surrounded Olivia. One man in that throng started yelling abuse at her about her team swap and called her a traitor. In a flash, he wielded a hammer at Olivia's head but missed. On his second attempt, Olivia remembered something Aleeza told her about close-quarter combat training. Attack the eyes. Olivia deflected his downward swinging arm long enough for her to shove her right thumb in his left eye socket and press firmly. 'Stand down or I'll gouge the eye out of your head,' Olivia warned.

The man screamed in pain as a security team finally intervened and wrestled the man to the ground. The attack visibly shook Olivia as her Lazzrini crew members quickly whisked her away.

Thirty minutes later, Olivia's PD buzzed.

'Hey, sweetie,' Nicolas Martin greeted as his holoimage beamed up from Olivia's PD. 'I just saw the news. Are you okay?'

'Yep. I think I came off better than he did,' Olivia replied. 'I'm just in the elevator going up to my room.'

'Are you sure you're okay?'

'I'm fine. The paramedics have checked me. I'm going to have a shower and then go out to dinner.'

'As long as you're okay. Jesus, there are some crazy fucking idiots out there.'

'Yep. I'm just glad I went into self-defence mode. I didn't even think about it, I just did.'

'I saw the footage. You were amazing, and you did. It looked like a natural reflex. Who taught you that?'

'Aleeza. I remember we did some self-defence stuff years ago.'

'Have you spoken to her?'

'She called, but I was busy.'

'You two need to talk to one another. She's your sister,' he said.

'Yeah. I'm at my floor, Dad, I have to go. Love you.' Olivia disconnected and stared at the numbers as the elevator ascended. Five more floors to go.

Later that evening, Henri Rossi sat up in bed in the luxury hotel room with his PD in hand and earfonic in one ear, watching a news report.

'A man wielding a hammer attacked Olivia Martin, the SkyRace GP maverick pilot,' the reporter began over drone footage of the incident, 'after she finished fourth in the Japanese SkyRace GP today. With some quick thinking on Ms Martin's part, the attacker was quickly overwhelmed and apprehended. On a happier note for Olivia Martin, it seems the skyracer had a torrid night on the town in Barcelona after the Spanish SkyRace GP. Finishing fifth in the event, ahead of her sister and now rival, Aleeza Martin, Olivia painted the town red with the renowned bad boy of Spanish fashion, Roberto Zapata.' Night vision footage of Olivia exiting Roberto Zapata's villa flashed to screen as the voiceover continued. 'A paparazzi drone captured Olivia Martin leaving the celebrity fashion designer's residence in the early hours.'

Henri placed his PD on the bedside table and removed his earfonic. 'Do you like to fuck?'

Olivia turned to face Henri, looking up at him. 'That's romantic.'

'Romance is fiction. Do you like to fuck?'

'Romance makes the world go round.'

'You know that romance is a primal human reproductive necessity, right? I am Italian, I know.'

'That is one of the most conceited, arrogant things I think I have ever heard you say, and you say a lot of arrogant shit, because you're a privileged, middle-aged white male.'

'Privileged white male, I will take. Middle-aged? Not quite.'

'It's a fact,' Olivia responded. 'Didn't you see the media conference today? Middle age starts at 35. You are middle-aged.'

'You think I am middle-aged?'

'Yes.'

Henri pondered that for a moment before he revived his line of reasoning. 'Let me give it a more accurate name, passion. Passion functions on a fundamental chemical reaction to create illusion, to create the initial stage of intimate excitement around the unknown. It is the psychological response that feeds the biological urge. After the endorphins have dissipated, the day-to-day reality kicks in.'

'When love kicks in.'

'Love is fulfilling, satisfying, a feeling of comfort and contentment. You like being in the presence of the other person to the point of commitment.'

'What are you saying, Henri?' Olivia questioned. 'Where is this leading?'

Henri studied her. 'I like to fuck.'

Olivia rolled over onto her back. 'So I've heard, with Italian actresses.'

'I assume you mean Greta Argento. Who told you?'

'I overheard a few of the crew talking. Have there been others in the short time we've been sharing a bed?'

'Have there been more than Roberto Zapata?' he countered.

Olivia remained silent. 'You saw the news feeds.'

'Paparazzi drones are everywhere these days.'

Olivia gave Henri a gentle smile. 'They are. I think we need a reset. We keep it purely professional from here on.'

'Agreed. I need to steer clear of female pilots again.'

'Agreed.' Olivia got out of bed and went into the ensuite, closing the door behind her.

Aleeza exited the ensuite of Bayden Turner's bedroom in his lavish apartment overlooking Hinokicho Park in Tokyo. She took her seat back at the dinner table as Bayden was serving a salted caramel baked cheesecake dessert.

'Thank you. So you have this exquisite kitchen, but you ordered in. You don't cook?'

'Occasionally, but not tonight. Just easier given my schedule today.'

'So you travel a lot?' She scooped up a spoonful of cake and devoured it.

'As much as you do. I'm on the road constantly. Luckily for me, Unicus owns an apartment like this in many cities.'

'So you do alright,' she teased.

'I manage.' He tasted the cheesecake. 'Mmmm, nice texture.'

'How long have you been with the Unicus Corporation?'

'Coming up to six years. I joined the corporation as their Chief Business Development Manager, then last year they offered me the Global Operations Manager's role. Before that I was with BMW as their International Brand Manager, overseeing the Dragonfly hoverbike launch.'

'Nice piece of machinery,' Aleeza commented. 'I have a D2600 in my garage in Vancouver.'

'E2800 P-Series in mine.' They exchanged smiles.

'Of course, you have the limited edition.'

'Maybe we use that in the commercial,' Bayden suggested. 'You and a hoverbike.'

'Have I agreed to do the commercial yet?' She challenged in jest. 'Have we settled on a fee?'

'No, sorry.'

'Where are you based in your down time?'

'Greenwich, Connecticut, when I can get there.'

'Did you grow up there?'

'No, no. I grew up in Boston.'

'Wife and kids in Greenwich? Sorry, sorry, I shouldn't be prying. It's none of my business.'

'No, it's okay. I have nothing to hide. Married and divorced, no children.'

'Me too.' Smiles rebounded again between the pair.

'You grew up in Victoria, British Columbia.'

'Yes, we are a family of pilots, except for Mum. She was a flight attendant with Air Canada. That's where my parents met.'

'Your mother died when you girls were in your teens?'

'You have done your homework. The doctors diagnosed her with ulcerative colitis, which progressed into colon cancer, and finally bowel cancer. She was only 41.'

'Is it hereditary?'

'No, but you probably know that, you know everything else about me. I crashed in Greece in '44. I found out in that hospital stay I was anaemic, like my mother. It causes fatigue, light-headedness, and that's what happened that day. I take supplements now to keep my dysfunctional red blood cells chugging along.' A brief pause in the conversation punctuated the balmy Tokyo night. 'So, should we talk more shop? That's why you flew me here.' She picked up her wineglass and sipped.

Bayden laughed at her accusation. 'No, you said you needed to get to Tokyo to fly home. That's why I offered you a lift.'

'Did I?'

'You did. Anyway, I pitched you everything in the aircar. I just wish we could splash the Empulsion brand across your racepod, helmet and racesuit like the good old days.'

'I don't know what it was like back then. My career started after the personal sponsorship ruling.'

'I started out in advertising, long before BMW, when the push for individual athletes not wanting to wear uniforms carrying certain sponsor's logos was gaining more and more momentum. Personal values infringement was the term they used. Back then, if a sponsor paid the club or team, everyone wore the branded gear as a blanket rule. Over time, fast food, energy drinks, gambling and alcohol companies dominated uniform sponsorship because they had the deepest pockets. The ruling was a sensible and mature approach, and I think the advertising revenue model that was brokered has benefited all parties. It wasn't a new model. The big four US sporting codes had been doing it for decades, just that the rest of the world was catching up. The decision meant athletes were no longer real estate to be sold to the highest bidder at the behest of the team owner.'

'To be honest, I don't know how I'd feel about being plastered with brands when I went out to compete. I think it would weigh me down, figuratively speaking,' Aleeza admitted. 'If my values didn't align with my sponsors, I'd find it stressful to put on a helmet and racesuit that promoted rubbish food or betting. When did that rule extend to the machines?'

'Not long after. Drivers and pilots associations united and gave team owners an ultimatum. If you want our drivers and pilots in your machines, which are an extension of the driver or pilot, vehicles are sponsor free zones as well. There was a strike for a few months, no races, and then team owners adjusted their sponsorship revenue model and everyone was onboard.'

'I remember the strike.'

'From that point forward, the event, the sporting code and broadcaster promoted the major sponsors, not the individual athlete.'

'I take it this is a passion of yours?'

'You think?' Bayden joked. 'It had a massive impact on sports sponsorship in the EU because I remember the argument that was being put forward, that entire sporting codes would collapse. It just didn't happen, and as you've pointed out, not having a slogan writ large down the sleeves of your racesuit removes that stress.'

'I love my designer racesuits.'

'I must admit, I really like some of your designer racesuits. Jun Mori aren't they?'

'Yep, from here in Tokyo.'

'I like the gold one, with the circulating blood in the veins between the metallic-looking plates.'

'Yep, one of my favourites this season.'

'We start the Empulsion premiumisation campaign in around four to six weeks. So, if you are good to go, I'll organise a shoot in Canada after the next race if that suits you.'

'Pushy.' She considered Bayden. 'I think my values align with the brand. I'm good to go. Keep me in the loop.'

'I will, and thank you. I'll send the contracts to Jericho for you to sign. And your fee?'

'How many stores are opening?'

'Six in major capital cities. Followed by another six in a few months.'

'Why stores and not online?'

'We're doing both, but our price points are high because our quality is superb. Research shows women love the opportunity to experience premium product in the flesh, shopping with friends is seen as an adventure, and they feel like they're getting expert advice first-hand. Statistics show premium clothing is first looked at online for inspiration, but 90 percent make the purchase in-store.'

'How much will each store sell in the first week?'

'Dollar wise? We've projected about $400,000.'

'My fee will be the total dollar amount generated by all six stores at the end of the first week. That's seven days, not five. And...I'll visit each store during that week to help promote the brand, at your expense.'

Bayden laughed. 'I love your idea for an in-store promotion, but you'll be tired by the end of that week.' Bayden considered her offer.

'I hope you have a warehouse full of product in each location.'

'We will.'

'Well?'

'Pushy... done. We are good to go.'

'Excellent. I'd better get going. I have a long way to travel to my hotel room.'

'Where are you staying?'

Aleeza pointed at the building across from the park, about 300 metres away.

'The Ritz? Really?'

'Really. You can walk me home.'

'Done.'

Chapter Five

Aleeza Martin and Brad Hazzard sat in business class en route to Riyadh, Saudi Arabia. Gordie and Jericho Starling sat behind them. Aleeza watched SEN TV on her PD with her earfonics in.

'In Fly Hard this week,' sportscaster Katie Kang began as vision played, 'a media release from Hoverflyers announced they have parted ways with technical director Kenny James following the Canadian SkyRace GP. The Leeds-based team has failed to place higher than ninth for the season in Division 1. James was contracted until the end of next season but was agreeable to a contract payout. They have not announced his replacement.'

'Due to a broken arm from a skiing accident, Floyd Hammer, the #1 pilot in Division 2, got ruled out of the upcoming Saudi Arabian GP, resulting in a reshuffle at Watson-Cruz Airsports. Watson-Cruz promoted Angel Greatorex to #1 pilot in Division 2. They also selected rookie Bernhard Kingston for the #2 spot in his debut.'

'The disqualification of Olivia Martin at the end of the Division 1 Canadian GP because of the width of her front wing exceeding regulation size was the start of a tough couple of weeks for the Lazzrini Race Team. A protest from the Lazzrini team saw an ugly altercation between Lazzrini's Team Principal, Sergio Pirozzi, and race stewards. Video of the extremely verbal dispute was widely shared on social media. Yesterday, we learnt things did not fare well for the Lazzrini Race Team after they were ordered to front the SkyRace GP Tribunal this week to face charges of bringing the sport into disrepute regarding that post-race protest incident. The Tribunal heavily fined the Lazzrini Race Team to the tune of $200,000 and docked them ten competition team points. Today is a different story and vindication has arrived for the Lazzrini team. Because of a data mix-up post-race, Olivia Martin was reinstated by the SkyRace GP Appeals Panel. She won the race in front of her home crowd and is now tied for the top spot on the Division 1 Pilot Standings with her sister, Aleeza Martin.'

'Fuck,' Aleeza said under her breath.

Gordie tapped Aleeza on the shoulder, prompting her to take out an earfonic. 'Have you seen the Empulsion ad yet?'

'Only a rough edit. Bayden said it might be out this week.'

'Turn your screen on, it's playing on the inflight channels.'

'Did you see they reinstated Olivia?'

'Yep. Have to grin and bear it. Watch your ad.'

Aleeza put her PD down and touched the menu console. As her monitor popped on, she replaced her earfonic and selected the audio output. She watched and waited for her commercial to come on.

The female voiceover began over a black screen fading up to slo-mo video of Aleeza approaching a hoverbike with helmet in hand wearing Empulsion designer activewear.

'As we navigate through the complexities of modern society, it's easy to get lost in the hustle and bustle of everyday life.' Vision cuts to Aleeza walking a mini schnauzer in a park. 'Our lifestyles are fast-paced and often leave us feeling tense and overwhelmed.' Vision cuts to Aleeza drinking coffee with a friend at an outdoor café in Rome. 'The psychological stress of negotiating interpersonal relationships, unpredictable setbacks, and increasing productivity in the workplace can lead to health issues.' Vision cuts to Aleeza working out in a gym. 'Taking control of your lifestyle is key to staying healthy and perceptive. Empulsion - Life and style combined.'

Cut to Aleeza standing beside her McRory racepod in Emulsion activewear. 'Empulsion. Good to go.'

Aleeza looked across at Brad, who was watching the commercial on her screen.

'What do you think?'

'Looks very polished. Do you like it?'

She thought about the question before she smiled. 'Yeah, I like it.' Her PD buzzed; it was her father. 'Hello, Dad.'

'Where are you?'

'On a flight to Riyadh.'

'I thought you might be in the air. Have you spoken to your sister?'

'I call her but she never responds,' came her honest answer. 'You saw how she acted in Vancouver; she wants nothing to do with me.'

'It breaks my heart to see you two like this. I don't know what's gotten into her. We can't let this situation continue between the two of you; we are family.'

'I know. But you saw how she reacted when she saw me at the table in the restaurant. She turned around and walked out. I think she'll be questioning her trust in you after surprising her like that.'

'I had to do something to get her to the table. When you get to the event, attempt to reach out to her.'

'I will,' Aleeza assured her father. 'Did you hear they reinstated her points after the Canadian win? We're equal first.'

'No, I didn't. Have to go, about to board.'

'Where are you headed?'

'Quebec. They need pilots to help fight the fires.'

'Be careful. I know how hard it is to fight fires from the air.'

'I know, I will. Take care and good luck. I love you.'

'Love you.' Aleeza disconnected and mulled over catching up with Olivia. She opened her PD contacts and tapped Olivia's image.

'Hi. Leave a message and I might get back to you,' Olivia's auto reply said before a beep signalled the start of the recording.

Aleeza remained quiet, then disconnected.

SkyRace GP Division 1 Pilot Standings after the Canadian event. Yellow indicates leader.

Location	Olivia	total	Aleeza	total	Lukas	total
USA	25 (1ˢᵗ)	119	20 (3ʳᵈ)	129	22 (2ⁿᵈ)	120
Spain	14 (5ᵗʰ)	133	11 (8ᵗʰ)	140	25 (1ˢᵗ)	145
Japan	18 (4ᵗʰ)	151	22 (2ⁿᵈ)	162	12 (7ᵗʰ)	157
Canada	25 (1ˢᵗ)	(151) 176	14 (5ᵗʰ)	176	13 (6ᵗʰ)	170

A couple of nights later, at a rooftop nightclub in Dubai, Olivia was living up to her pre-race reveller moniker. Olivia was an enigmatic yet popular figure, a master of the art of partying. She exuded confidence, charm, and charisma, and was always the life of the party. Olivia knew how to have a good time and was skilled at creating an atmosphere of fun and excitement wherever she went with her expanding entourage. Her energy was contagious, and her ability to socialise with ease set her apart from the crowd. Her fashion and style choices had shifted to the next level as she mixed with famous designers, influencers, musicians, and actors. She possessed a powerful mix of courage, wit and charm, which drew people towards her.

The next morning, hungover, she caught a flight to Riyadh and then a connecting shuttle quadcopter to the SkyRace GP circuit 50 kilometres southeast of Riyadh.

Days later, Aleeza followed closely behind Jing Zhao, the #1 pilot for XPang-Fu Race Team, and Tamas Hutlassa, Air Schneider's #1 pilot, during the last lap of the Saudi Arabian GP.

'...Aleeza Martin sits at the back of the second pack as they battle it out in the concluding kilometres of this final lap,' SEN sportscaster Harvie Stedman explained. 'Olivia Martin is behind her and both are unlikely to get a podium finish at this late stage. Rita Perez is currently leading Aimee Walton-Dewa, with Matilda Vettel and Kawano Takayuki battling it out for third and fourth. The leading four racepods tackle the last bend! Here they come towards the finish line, pushing their racepods to breaking point, but it looks like Rita Perez will hold on to claim victory over Aimee Walton-Dewa and Kawano Takayuki has pipped Matilda Vettel for third. A very close race and now the second pack finishes with Aleeza Martin placing seventh and behind them, Olivia Martin in eighth and Lukas de Castro in ninth. Let's bring up the pilot standings, and we have a new outright leader! Aleeza has knocked her sister out of the top spot and now leads by a single point, with Lukas de Castro still holding third position. McRory Racing continue to lead the team standings with Lazzrini in second.'

SkyRace GP Division 1 Pilot Standings after the Saudi Arabian event. Yellow indicates leader.

Location	Olivia	total	Aleeza	total	Lukas	total
USA	25 (1st)	119	20 (3rd)	129	22 (2nd)	120
Spain	14 (5th)	133	11 (8th)	140	25 (1st)	145
Japan	18 (4th)	151	22 (2nd)	162	12 (7th)	157
Canada	25 (1st)	(151) 176	14 (5th)	176	13 (6th)	170
Saudi Arabia	11 (8th)	187	12 (7th)	188	5 (9th)	175

That night, in an apartment in Riyadh, Aleeza entered the living room wearing a plush white bath robe having just showered. She plopped down on the lush leather lounge beside Bayden Turner.

'Look at this,' Bayden gestured to the wall screen. 'Water bombing aircraft crashed in Quebec, killing both crew.'

It immediately caught Aleeza's attention. 'What? Turn it up!'

'Relax, it was an Australian crew. They clipped a tree.'

'Fuck! don't do that. You scared me. My heart is in my mouth.'

'Sorry,' he apologised. 'I know your father's in Quebec doing the same thing, but I wouldn't have mentioned it if I didn't know who died.' He let the prickly air settle before continuing. 'I didn't think you would want to go down to the restaurant, so I ordered dinner from the room service menu.'

'Well done, Mr Turner.' She gazed at him. 'You know we have to keep this indiscretion quiet, don't you?' Aleeza half asked, half told him.

'I assumed that was the idea.'

'I thought our Canadian thing was going to be a one-off, you know, but—'

'Here we are again.'

She fell into his eyes. 'Here we are again.'

'Does it bother you we're here again?' He softly questioned, brushing damp hair away from her eyes with his index finger.

'Does it bother you?'

'I asked first.'

She pondered the question. 'I can be myself around you. I like that. It's hard to relax, cause I'm always on, being in the public eye. But you, Mr Turner, you seem to have a calming effect on me. I love our banter.'

'Good. I feel the same. This feels unforced, comfortable. I feel content.'

Aleeza leaned in and tenderly kissed his lips. 'Ditto.'

'I want to show you my house in Greenwich.'

Aleeza sat back. 'Didn't we just agree we needed to be discrete?'

'Sure, but we can fly in and out without a fuss for a weekend. Nothing public.'

'When? I have to be in Egypt on the 2nd.'

'So we have a couple of weeks. Check your diary and see if you can make it next week.'

A knock at the door interrupted the conversation. 'That will be dinner.' Bayden got up to open the door. 'Let's discuss it over some authentic Arabian cuisine.'

The Fly Hard graphic flashed to the screen as its signature music played on the wall screen in Olivia's hotel room. She rushed about adding the finishing touches to her outfit, accessories and make-up for a night on the town in Riyadh. An invitation only secret dance club called The Emerald Oasis was her destination. According to reports, wealthy Saudi royal family members frequented the club, which served alcohol and designer dance drugs.

'In Fly Hard this week we have a special report on party pilot, Olivia Martin,' commentator Katie Kang reported, over social media footage of Olivia in full party mode.

Olivia instantly stopped what she was doing to watch the program.

'She revolves from one party to the next with sometimes embarrassing results and this is causing headaches for Lazzrini bosses as whispers grow louder from SkyRace GP central on how they're going to rein her in. Others, namely her millions of fans, are calling her a breath of fresh air for the SkyRace brand and her fanbase has grown exponentially. But before we get to that story, let's catch up on other news.'

'Fuck you gossipmonger, Katty Kang. If the fans like it, that's all that matters.' She continued her preparation.

'After the violent attack on Olivia Martin at the end of the Japanese GP,' vision of the incident played, 'the rights holder of the SkyRace GP, Deltop Media Group, will trial two dozen P-droid series security robots supplied by Pearl Stemthetics at the upcoming Egyptian Grand Prix.' Footage showed the humanoid P-droids in a variety of security roles. 'The Chairman and largest shareholder of the Deltop Media Group, the recluse Ted Pearl, and Chairman of Pearl Stemthetics, has donated the units at no cost. It took several rounds of negotiations to approve the use of the new Protection-droids at the event, but in the end, all parties came to an agreement. Pearl Stemthetics are the manufacturer of semi-autonomous synthetic humanoids. A couple of years ago, Pearl Stemthetics introduced the O-droid series for dangerous industrial occupations, and they recently released the P-droid series for personal security. The P-droid security guards will not carry firearms and be under strict supervision from human security personnel to monitor crowds during the event. If the trial is successful, they will be deployed at all future SkyRace GP events.'

The following weekend, Aleeza alighted Bayden Turner's Bugatti Aurora aircar in the courtyard of his Greenwich home. Surrounded by forest, she stared at the impressive house. 'Did you buy this place with your wife?'

'Yep. I was still at BMW. Twelve years ago, yeah, about '36.'

'Beautiful house and aspect. So big for two people.'

'I thought so, too. But she wanted to do the whole weekend dinner party thing with guests staying over. Come on, I'll show you the lake.' They walked down a gravel path from the aircar landing pad. 'We were only together for a few years.'

'And you got the house?'

'I paid for it and we had a prenup. She walked away wealthier, believe me.'

The path opened onto a small timber jetty. 'Do you have a boat?'

'No. It's a manmade reservoir, not a natural lake. I've got a kayak that I never use.'

They wandered back to the house. 'So, you must have a pool.'

'Used to. We landed on where it used to be. I'm not here enough to use a pool, so I turned it into a landing pad.'

'As you do. So, why did you keep it?'

'The house? Seclusion, solitude. It's my insulation from my fast world.'

'You think your world is fast?' Aleeza mocked.

'It has a traditional theatre, Holoflix room, VRXLR8 deck, gym, wine cellar, billiards and games room, golf driving range, sauna, spa—'

'Okay, okay, so you just like to lie low here when you can.'

'Exactly.' They entered the main house with its sweeping staircase and marble floor foyer.

'Fuck! This is impressive,' Aleeza gushed. 'How do you maintain this place?'

'A small army that costs me a shitload.'

'I bet. Have you ever thought about downsizing?'

'Spend a few days here and then ask me.'

'I haven't pried until now, but tell me, why did you get divorced?'

'Short version, I was away a lot on business. She got lonely and had an affair. I can't blame her. That's my life.'

'Hmmm. Show me the house while I digest that.'

On the morning of the Egyptian Grand Prix Division 1 race, unseasonal rain threatened the event. Aleeza called a pilots' meeting to gauge their concerns about flying in rain clutter.

Rain and racepods flying at hundreds of kilometres an hour in close proximity don't go well together. Speed is the reason. Raindrops absorb and scatter radar and LiDAR signals, so less energy reaches the target and even less returns to radar as an echo. Radar clutter is unwanted rain reflections that mix with aircraft echoes and hinder target detection. Initially, water droplets and vapor absorb electromagnetic energy, resulting in a loss of radar signal. Second, rain produces a return signal that obstructs radar information and conceals targets. The phenomenon is known as rain clutter and poses a serious risk to pilots if their instruments are compromised.

After speaking with the pilots, Aleeza and Morgan Patel, #2 pilot from the AeroWing Aviation team, went to see Perry Calver, the SkyRace GP Race Director, to discuss a postponement or cancelation of the race because of precipitation. Perry told them he would urgently call a Race Committee meeting and then an all pilots' meeting in 15 minutes.

'Thanks for joining us at short notice,' Perry Calver addressed all the pilots. 'Aleeza and Morgan told us there were concerns about racing in the rain. Safety is all of our concern; we all have that responsibility. We've consulted with the local meteorological department and a few other sources and all are indicting the rain will be short-lived, an hour at the most. The Race Committee has postponed the qualifying sprints for an hour, but we want to continue moving forward with the event.'

'How does everyone feel about that?' Aleeza posed the question to her colleagues. Muttering spread throughout the group. 'As Perry said, safety is everyone's responsibility, but you are the people putting your lives on the line. You have the final say to whether you fly today. This is not a Race Committee decision. I think we need a show of hands if you want to fly after a postponement. Hands up if–'

'Can I say something before we vote?' Olivia interrupted. 'If we vote not to fly today, that reduces the number of remaining races, which will affect the points at the end of the season. That may benefit some pilots in this season's championship. Just putting it out there.'

Aleeza shot Olivia a frosty glare before the vote was taken. The majority of pilots voted for the event to go ahead after the postponement.

By the time the main event had begun, the rain had passed as forecast. The late qualifying sprints agitated the crowd and cast a cautious mood over the teams.

Olivia pushed ahead of Aleeza, who both started in the second row of the grid, well behind Lukas de Castro, who started from pole. Aleeza narrowed the gap between the fifth and six lap but felt something wasn't right with her front right rotor housing. As she attempted to bear down on Olivia, she crossed the exhaust wake from Olivia's rear thruster and that resulted in the front right rotor housing on her racepod to shudder. In a split second, Aleeza lost control and crashed into the embankment without sending a mayday call. It all happened so rapidly.

'Accident alert, accident alert, rescue vehicle en route,' the Race Traffic Controller warned through Olivia's helmet comms system.

'Aleeza, do you copy?' Gordie's stressed voice asked over the comms.

'Copy, Gordie,' she replied groggily. 'I'm here.' After her airbags deflated, she took off her helmet and released her harness. She felt her left wrist and her monkey bracelet was gone. She quickly searched below the throttle bracket, but couldn't find it. Aleeza stood on her seat and waved toward the SkyRing airship, knowing the cameras would be on her. She surveyed the dry riverbed before she attempted to get out of her cockpit, still lightheaded from the crash. Her leading foot caught the cockpit rubber seal as she tried to step out and her momentum propelled her forward. As if in slow motion, with an outstretched left hand, Aleeza fell onto rocks. She heard the crack of bone in her wrist, immediately eclipsed by an angry shot of pain across her forearm. Her arm collapsed; the dull thud of her head striking a smooth rock was the last insult in the calamitous mishap.

Several minutes later, the rescue crew found Aleeza unconscious in a crumpled heap beside her racepod. They immediately airlifted her to a Luxor hospital.

An hour later, Aleeza rested on a hospital gurney in an ER after arm and head x-rays. Her arm was being prepped for an operation. Her PD buzzed. 'Can you check that?'

Gordie grabbed her PD. 'It's Olivia. R U OK?'

'That's a big effort, texting to see how her sister is doing. Where did she finish?'

'Third, behind Jing. De Castro won.'

'Puts her back on top of the standings.'

'Yep. Do you want me to reply?'

'Text her I died. See if that gets a response.'

Gordie tilted his head and gave her a questioning look. 'Erm, no.' He put her PD in his pocket.

'We ready now,' the ER nurse explained in broken English. 'Surgeon explain procedure.'

The female surgeon smiled at Aleeza before she explained the procedure in Arabic.

After listening, the nurse interpreted the information. 'Thirty minute operation. Insert distal radial plate on radius bone. Distal radius fracture take three months to better. Full recover take one year.'

'A year!' Aleeza exclaimed. 'Gordie, I can't be out for a year.'

'We'll get a second opinion as soon as we get back to Vancouver, but your wrist needs to be set now for the fastest recovery.'

The nurse resumed interpreting as the surgeon continued. 'After surgery, feel little pain, ache, swelling in wrist. Take drugs.'

'Is this the best option to repair the fracture?' Aleeza asked the surgeon.

The nurse interpreted, then listened carefully to the surgeon's response. 'Yes. Common break, best option. Fast recovery.' She started to push the gurney. 'No worry, good doctor.'

'I'll be here when you wake up,' Gordie reassured her with a pat on the shoulder as she passed by.

SkyRace GP Division 1 Pilot Standings after the Egyptian event. Yellow indicates leader.

Location	Olivia	total	Aleeza	total	Lukas	total
USA	25 (1st)	119	20 (3rd)	129	22 (2nd)	120
Spain	14 (5th)	133	11 (8th)	140	25 (1st)	145
Japan	18 (4th)	151	22 (2nd)	162	12 (7th)	157
Canada	25 (1st)	(151) 176	14 (5th)	176	13 (6th)	170
Saudi Arabia	11 (8th)	187	12 (7th)	188	5 (9th)	175
Egypt	20 (3rd)	207	DNF	188	25 (1st)	200

Aleeza woke in a private hospital room. Gordie sat in a chair by the window, tapping the PD in his hand.

'How did it go?' Aleeza croaked.

'Ah, you're awake. Well, yes, the surgeon said it went well.' He helped her have a sip of water. 'Just texting Olivia telling her you're out of surgery. She started texting me, so I gave in.'

At that moment, Bayden Turner walked through the door. 'I came as soon as I heard.'

'I'll give you a minute,' Gordie excused himself from the room.

'How are you feeling?' He held her good hand.

'I had a fall,' Aleeza pouted. 'I've got a massive lump on the side of my head.'

'Yes, everyone saw it happen live.'

'Fuck,' came her deflated reaction. 'More fodder for memes.'

'There are some very creative memes already,' he teased, stroking her arm. 'I was thinking, you'll need to stay put for a while. I'm owed some vacation. You want to come play house with me in Greenwich? I can take care of you.'

Aleeza searched his face. She thought he had a kind face. 'I'm good to go when you are.'

Gordie looked through the small window in the door before entering. 'Aleeza, it's your father. Want to talk to him?'

'Sure.'

Three weeks later, Aleeza laid across a king-sized smart bed recuperating in Bayden's Greenwich house. The Mexico SkyRace GP was live on the bedroom wall screen, the sound muted. Matilda Vettel won the event for X Force with AeroWing's Royce Simms in second and Kawano Takayuki from Hoverflyers in third. Aleeza watched as Olivia, who finished fourth, was being interviewed by Harvie Stedman from SEN TV. She stared at her sister, who hadn't been in contact with her since the text message in the Luxor hospital in Egypt. Olivia maintained her #1 position on the pilot standings, according to the graphic at the bottom of the screen.

Aleeza's PD buzzed; it was her specialist. She put him on speaker. 'Vincent, I hope you've got good news for me?'

'Hi, Aleeza. Positive news. The fracture is regenerating very well from the scan you sent through this morning. The low-intensity NIR stimulation is working.'

'Excellent.'

'If you maintain the nutrient-rich diet with minimal arm movement, the fracture will be strong enough to make the South African GP in five weeks.'

'Not good enough, Vincent. I want to compete in Türkiye in three weeks.'

'Aleeza, that is only six weeks recovery, not long enough for the fracture to heal sufficiently before you subject it to the extreme physical exertion for two plus hours. It could do long-term damage,' her doctor advised.

'It's my throttle hand, not the joystick. I'd agree if it was my joystick hand.'

'I don't agree. You constantly grip the throttle throughout the race, and it may require more sustained tension than the joystick.'

Aleeza thought about her doctor's argument. 'Can we increase the near infrared stimulation sessions?'

He paused before answering. 'Look, I won't sign-off on you getting back in the cockpit when you aren't fit. If you were a schoolteacher or office worker, I'd say yes to six weeks recovery before returning to work, but you're a skyracer, an occupation that requires strong wrists over a prolonged period–'

'Vincent, you didn't answer my question.'

He let out a heavy sigh. 'We can increase the low-intensity NIR to daily sessions, but I can't guarantee you'll be ready for Türkiye in three weeks.'

'What time should I be there tomorrow?'

'Be here at 11.' He disconnected.

'Bayden!' Aleeza called. 'Bayden! Where are you?' She went off to look for him.

'In the office,' came the distant reply.

'I need to be in New York tomorrow for another appointment with Vincent,' she said, entering his office. 'Can I borrow your aircar? I thought you were on vacation?'

'I am, just keeping my finger on the Empulsion pulse. It's been extremely well received thanks to you.' He came around his desk. 'You don't have to ask to borrow it.' He took her hand. 'I've been thinking. Do you like it here?'

Aleeza gave him a curious look. 'Yeess,' came her drawn out response. 'Why?'

'How would you feel if we made this a permanent thing?'

'How exactly? Explain yourself, Mr Turner.'

'Well,' he placed her hand in his right hand and covered it with his left hand. 'Can I take your hand in marriage?'

'What! Take my hand in marriage? Are we in the 1800s? Who says take your hand in marriage?'

'So you remember this moment,' he said with honesty.

Aleeza stared at him with a grin. 'You're right, I will remember this moment.'

'Well?'

She continued to stare. 'It's been a whirlwind courtship, Mr Turner. We have both been wed before and both failed due to lack of commitment and infidelity.'

'Yes, but–'

Aleeza put her index finger against his lips. 'I would be honoured for you to take my hand, fine sir.' They kissed. 'I would love to spend my life with you and grow old together.'

'Thank you. When?' Bayden questioned.

'Are you sure? Have you thought this through?'

'When will you be back in the air?'

'Three weeks for Türkiye.'

'What?' Bayden reacted with concern. 'Is that what Vincent said?'

'He said he couldn't guarantee it, but we're working towards that timeframe.'

'It seems too soon after a wrist fracture,' Bayden suggested.

'I didn't know you had a medical degree?'

'I thought it was eight weeks, minimum?'

'He said the infrared stimulation has been really positive.'

'Okay. So, should we do it before or after the Türkiye GP?'

'Before. Something very low key away from media, secret even, here, yeah?'

'Sure. Will you invite Olivia?'

'Of course, she's my sister.'

SkyRace GP Division 1 Pilot Standings after the Mexican event. Yellow indicates leader.

Location	Olivia	total	Aleeza	total	Lukas	total
USA	25 (1st)	119	20 (3rd)	129	22 (2nd)	120
Spain	14 (5th)	133	11 (8th)	140	25 (1st)	145
Japan	18 (4th)	151	22 (2nd)	162	12 (7th)	157
Canada	25 (1st)	(151) 176	14 (5th)	176	13 (6th)	170
Saudi Arabia	11 (8th)	187	12 (7th)	188	5 (9th)	175
Egypt	20 (3rd)	207	DNF	188	25 (1st)	200
Mexico	18 (4th)	225	Withdrawn	188	14 (5th)	214

Chapter Six

The McRory Racing crew applauded Aleeza as she sauntered into Barney's for breakfast on Wednesday morning before the Türkiye SkyRace GP southeast of Karapinar. She took a bow before she selected her chicken, vegetables and pasta from the bain-marie and sat down beside Dylan.

'Welcome back. We missed you,' Dylan told her. 'Congratulations on the wedding.'

'Thanks. Great to be back.'

'I have something for you.' Dylan reached into the chest pocket of his grubby blue overalls. 'Hold out your hand.'

Aleeza eyeballed him, as pranks were not uncommon between the pair. She obeyed and held out her right hand. Dylan dropped her monkey bracelet into her palm. 'You found it! Thank you, Dylan.'

'It was broken, so I had it repaired.'

'Wow! Thank you.' She gave him a one-armed hug. 'I'll have to put it on my right wrist for now.' She held up her left forearm, protected in a thermoplastic wrist brace. 'Can you put it on?' She gave back the bracelet so he could put it around her right wrist.

'How is your wrist?'

'Getting there. Still got the plate screwed to the bone, probably have that in there for a few months. Got some race approved painkillers so I'm good to go.'

Friday's circuit practise was as hectic as usual. The volcanic desert region in Türkiye, south of Karapinar, was a well-known tourist destination. Away from known earthquake zones, this Grand Prix always proved to be a major draw card for European fans. This sky circuit was also unique because it incorporated the obstacles. In a section of the circuit, pilots had to fly through a seven metre long metal tube, immediately followed by a 25 metre vertical metal hurdle, back down through a second seven metre metal tube and finally over a 15 metre hurdle. Three sets of obstacles sat side-by-side, so pilots had to compete for alignment with the five meter diameter tubes. Arriving first posed no problem, but more than three racepods meant slowing down and waiting their turn. These obstacles were unforgiving if hit.

Olivia had just finished her practise session when she saw her sister walking towards her out the corner of her eye. She turned away and pretended to be busy, speaking with a Lazzrini crew member.

'Olivia, can I talk to you?'

Olivia turned around. 'Sure.'

'You didn't reply to my wedding invitation. Dad was really disappointed you weren't there. You told him you were coming.'

'I can't be responsible for how he feels.'

'I felt hurt and disappointed.' The distance between them was only a few metres, but it felt like a canyon to Aleeza.

'I'll come to the next one,' Olivia heartlessly told her.

'Why didn't you come?' Aleeza waited for a reply that never came. 'What the fuck is wrong with you? What happened between us? You didn't come to the hospital even after this happened.' She held up her injured arm. 'This is a job, Olivia; we fly for different teams but it's just a job. In a few years this will all end and—'

'And what? We'll still be sisters and live happily ever after? This is more than a job for me, Aleeza. What you said to me concerning the recording of Brad started this. Then you fucking said it publicly, adding fuel to the fire.'

'Fuck you! No, Olivia! Don't you throw this back on me. You foolishly releasing the recording started this. I just responded to your idiot act. You didn't think of the repercussions. You never have. Even when you were little, you blindly did what you wanted without thinking about others.'

Olivia took a step towards her sister. 'You always got your own way. You manipulated me when we were kids. If you wanted to do something or to eat something or say something to hurt someone, you suggested it to me and I did the asking or telling. You controlled me like a puppet for years. I was the one who got into trouble from what you suggested I do. I did it, so I got the blame for it. You were the responsible older sister. I was always the fucking loose cannon.' Tears rolled down her cheeks. 'Brad tried to stop me from chasing a dream and you never once took my side. You never have. Even when we were kids, you sided with mum and dad. I have always had your back, always, but you left me to−' she paused. 'I'm not having this argument with you again.' She turned to walk away, but stopped to face Aleeza. 'And by the way, I don't need a sister anymore.' She disappeared inside the pit hangar.

Tears welled in Aleeza's eyes. Before anyone could see them spill down her face, she walked away, overcome, concealing the intense knot of unease wedged in her chest.

As night fell, crowds swelled in the cafes and bars. A vibrant atmosphere filled the air, buzzing with excitement and anticipation. People gathered in groups, laughing and chatting, enjoying the company of friends. Patrons queued anxiously, waiting their turn to order their favourite beverage. In one crowded bar, an inebriated young man abruptly pushed his way into a line, causing a commotion among the other people waiting patiently. The unruly individual seemed to have no regard for the rules or the patience of others. A scuffle broke out and security was immediately called. Two uniformed P-droids arrived with their handler less than a minute later. Amidst the chaos, the troublemaker brandished a broken bottle in a menacing manner towards his attackers. The atmosphere, once lively and convivial, quickly turned tense as patrons and staff alike watched on. The security guard, trained to handle such situations, swiftly took action to protect himself and others from harm. With a calm yet assertive demeanour, the guard confidently ordered both the grey-faced P-droids to disarm the inebriated man in a safe manner. Working with precision as a team, the P-droids effectively neutralised him. One P-droid pointed its index finger at the wrist of the hand holding the bottle. A short electric arc sparked and crackled, compelling the offender to drop it, as the second P-droid simultaneously sweep kicked the man's feet out from under him. They dragged him out of the establishment by his legs, to loud cheers and claps from the appreciative crowd.

Aleeza strolled by the bar as the P-droids were ejecting the nuisance. Her mind was elsewhere; it had wandered off on a ruminating tangent. She was concerned about her altercation with her sister. Questions kept swirling through her head. *Was she really that terrible as a sister?* She was worried about the impact that her new marital status would have on her performance. She now had a great deal to lose if she took unnecessary risks. *Would she lose her uncompromising edge and become vulnerable as a pilot? Was her wrist going to be up to the stress of the race?*

Brad Hazzard and his wife were also out, soaking up the carnival atmosphere. 'Aleeza!' Brad called.

Aleeza was a million kilometres from where she was. She looked at Brad and Astrid without seeing them at first. 'Oh, hi. Sorry, lost in thought.'

'Tell her,' Astrid quickly prompted her husband.

'I finish up with McRory at the end of the season,' Brad reported matter-of-factly. 'They aren't renewing my contract.'

'What? Was that what Jericho and Gordie wanted to discuss?'

'Yep.'

'Jesus, Brad,' Aleeza uttered, glancing at Astrid. 'I'm so sorry to hear that. What are you going to do?'

'I've already got a meeting with Air Schneider tomorrow.'

'Well, that's positive, I suppose. Wow, I can't believe they didn't renew your contract. What are they thinking?'

'They made it painfully obvious that Max did a better job than me while replacing you in Mexico. Sounds like they'll promote him to D1 next year.'

'They're arseholes,' Astrid expressed. 'Did you speak to Olivia?'

'Tried to. She shits me.'

'She missed out on a beautiful wedding. How's the wrist after practise?' Astrid queried.

Aleeza looked down at her encased wrist. 'It held up okay, better than I thought it would.'

'Sunday will be the genuine test,' Brad said. 'Is Bayden coming?'

'Flying in on Sunday morning.'

'Have you eaten? We're going to grab something,' Brad half invited.

'No, I don't have much of an appetite at the moment. I think I'll keep walking.'

'Welcome, everyone, to the Türkiye SkyRace Division 1 Grand Prix,' Katie Kang announced to her worldwide audience. 'The weather is absolutely brilliant this Sunday morning and Aleeza Martin is back! Aleeza Martin got married to Bayden Turner, the Global Operations Manager for the Unicus Corporation, during her brief hiatus. We hope to see her trademark style of flying hard on display today, because what a difference one race makes. Aleeza has slipped back to a distant third from a close third position behind Lukas de Castro and her sister Olivia Martin, sitting pretty at number one.'

'Yes, Katie,' Harvie Stedman, her co-sportscaster, chimed in. 'I'm amazed Aleeza is back racing so soon. Given only six weeks ago, she fractured her wrist in that bizarre accident in Egypt, getting out of her ra~ od after she crashed. I hope her wrist is up to the rigours of flying ~r two solid hours, because as you know, Katie, pilots' bodies are constantly under stress, stretching and compressing as they experience the G forces that come with hard banking manoeuvres.'

'And the occasional barrel roll,' Katie Kang added. 'Yes, Harvie, I'm all too familiar with the stress the body is put under during a race. Now, after the sprint qualifying session earlier, Aleeza Martin will start in the second row on the grid with Lukas de Castro in poll position along with Tamas Hutlassa and Rita Perez. Olivia Martin is in the unenviable position of twelfth, fourth row of the grid.'

The constant stress on Aleeza's recovering left wrist during the race made it ache, even with painkillers. The twinges started Friday during the practise session and were ever present through the earlier sprint qualifying. Despite her determination to push through the pain, the relentless movement, vibration and shuddering of her racepod only intensified the discomfort. Every throttle change she made sent sharp waves of agony up her arm, an ever-present reminder of the injury. The hurt was a constant companion, a dull throb that refused to subside, no matter how much she tried to ignore it.

As the race progressed, the ache seemed to spread, engulfing her entire arm. It radiated from her wrist, travelling up to her elbow and beyond. Each throttle correction became an exercise in stamina, as she battled against both her competitors and the relentless pain. Every twist and turn of the course exacerbated the agony, as if the universe were conspiring against her. She gritted her teeth, determined not to let her damaged wrist hinder her performance. The mental strain of the race combined with the physical anguish created a perfect storm of discomfort. Yet, she refused to give in, pushing through the agony with sheer willpower.

Aleeza had her radio mic and cockpit camera switched off, only listening to Gordie's directions and updates, so no one heard her groans, a steady stream of expletives or witness her grimaces. Deep down, she knew the toll that the constant stress was taking on her. The torment was not just physical, but also a reminder of her vulnerability. It served as a humbling reminder that something as simple as a broken bone can bring even the strongest down.

Towards the end of the race, Olivia, behind Aleeza, became increasingly frustrated, so she began to take risks. On her last lap, she approached the obstacles. She was flying in a pack of four and unwilling to yield her position. Olivia glanced to her left; Brad Hazzard was beside her, aligning his racepod for the far right tube. Olivia needed to get there first. Both pilots accelerated. Brad was in the better position to enter the tube squarely, Olivia was not. Time had run out; the rules stipulate that the inside racepod has right of way in this situation and the outside racepod must give way and wait. Olivia didn't wait and flew underneath Brad's racepod as they were about to enter the tube, a tube designed for a single racepod. Her front right rotor housing clipped the tube entrance and smashed. Olivia's racepod hit the tube floor and slid. Audio proximity warnings in Brad's cockpit wailed as he accurately inched his racepod up just enough to keep out of her way. His left rotor housing scraped along the inside of the tube. Momentum carried Olivia out of the tube and into the sand, where she came to rest. She punched the cockpit canopy in frustration.

'Good riddance,' Brad muttered as he saw her failure captured through his rear facing camera while climbing towards the 25 metre high hurdle.

'Accident alert, accident alert, rescue vehicle en route,' the Race Traffic Controller warned through Aleeza's helmet comms system.

Aleeza wanted the pain to be over. She checked her Ghost Pod interface for her current position and 'projected' speed in order to win the race. Although her left forearm trembled, she nudged her throttle to fly faster. She overtook Dirk Alberts in the Vogel Machina racepod for the lead in the home straight.

'Oz has crashed,' Gordie informed her over comms.

Aleeza couldn't help herself. She switched her mic on. 'Is she alright?'

'All good. No injuries.'

As Aleeza crossed the finish line, a mixture of relief and exhaustion washed over her. The race was finally over, and with it, the relentless tension on her wrist. She couldn't help but feel a sense of accomplishment, knowing that she had overcome not only her competitors, but also the constant torment that had plagued her throughout the race. She glanced at the monkey bracelet on her right wrist with a smile.

'What a comeback for Aleeza Martin!' Harvie Stedman exclaimed to the world. 'And her last lap was the race fastest! Wow!'

'Hey, it looks like you picked up an extra point for fastest lap,' Gordie told her. 'Good to have you back.'

Now, as she permitted herself a moment of respite, Aleeza couldn't resist contemplating how long it would take for her wrist to heal completely. The grief served as a reminder that her recovery journey was far from over, and that she would need patience and dedication to fully mend and regain her strength. In the end, the constant stress on her damaged wrist during the race had taken its toll. It had made her ache, both physically and emotionally. But it had also taught her valuable lessons about resilience and the indomitable spirit of the human will. Aleeza knew she still possessed that desire to win, and she would emerge from this ordeal stronger than ever before.

'I am in awe of this woman, Harvie,' Katie Kang revered. 'Her tenacity and courage to not only return so quickly after a wrist fracture but then persevere to win, you have to admire the intestinal fortitude of the woman. I'm sure her wrist would have been giving her some grief, but we never heard a word from her over comms. Her unwavering determination to finish first is a symbol of strength and endurance, a testament to a staunch champion's spirit.'

SkyRace GP Division 1 Pilot Standings after the Türkiye event. Yellow indicates leader.

location	Olivia	total	Aleeza	total	Lukas	total
USA	25 (1ˢᵗ)	119	20 (3ʳᵈ)	129	22 (2ⁿᵈ)	120
Spain	14 (5ᵗʰ)	133	11 (8ᵗʰ)	140	25 (1ˢᵗ)	145
Japan	18 (4ᵗʰ)	151	22 (2ⁿᵈ)	162	12 (7ᵗʰ)	157
Canada	25 (1ˢᵗ)	(151) 176	14 (5ᵗʰ)	176	13 (6ᵗʰ)	170
Saudi Arabia	11 (8ᵗʰ)	187	12 (7th)	188	5 (9ᵗʰ)	175
Egypt	20 (3ʳᵈ)	207	DNF	188	25 (1ˢᵗ)	200
Mexico	18 (4ᵗʰ)	225	Withdrawn	188	14 (5ᵗʰ)	214
Türkiye	DNF	225	25 (1st) +1	214	13 (6ᵗʰ)	227

Olivia and a well-dressed, attractive man emerged from The Sanctuary nightclub in Cape Town at 2 am to a loitering pack of paparazzi drones hovering at streetlight level. The pair had ditched her entourage and jumped into a waiting RoboCab van.

'Destination?' the feminine voice of the autonomous vehicle enquired.

'Where are you staying?' the man asked Olivia.

Olivia thought for a moment. 'Erm, Table Bay Hotel?'

'Table Bay Hotel,' he repeated.

'What was your name again?' Olivia questioned.

'Darius.'

Olivia stared at him through glazed eyes. 'Yes, Darius. You're a fine specimen, Darius.' She grabbed his face with both hands and drew him in for a moist kiss.

The next morning, about 140 kilometres northeast of Cape Town, the South African SkyRace GP transient township had risen from the dirt. The South African sky circuit boasted the air gate challenge for pilots. Some liked it, most hated it. This was a series of vertical air gates that created a four kilometre snaking slalom. Each gate comprised two cone-shaped pylons, which were 25 meters high and spaced seven meters apart. Each gate was positioned 100 metres apart, with 40 in total. The PVC-coated nylon used to create the inflatable air gates was pliant to prevent major harm to racepods, but a direct collision would cause serious consequences. Each pylon recorded the slightest contact by a racepod at speed via base lasers blanketing the entire surface of the pylon. Interrupt that laser barrier, even a scratch, and the pylon recorded an impact. They were sturdy enough to remain stationary in windy conditions of up to 5o km/h. Knowing where the wind was coming from was vital as they approached each air gate to allow for and negotiate the drift of the racepod. The twisting course required needle-like focus from pilots to thread themselves through the gates, because each gate hit added five seconds to a pilot's overall time. The air gates slowed all pilots down, but most made it through unscathed.

After finishing breakfast at Barney's, Aleeza booked a slot on one of the Reality XLR8 racepod simulators. Her Wednesday ritual hadn't faltered all season. She had followed the same routine for months and had seen the results in her last race. She was confident that her wrist physiotherapy between races was paying off and felt positive going into this weekend's race.

When the race started, Aleeza flew off the grid from poll, maintained her lead position and stuck to her race plan. She kept her composure and stayed ahead of the pack. Aleeza was especially competent at navigating the air gate section. By the end, Aleeza had flown a very strategic race and finished second, well ahead of Lukas de Castro and Olivia.

As they approached the finish line, Jing Zhao in his XPang-Fu racepod swooped down in front of Olivia, startling her out of complacency. She was light years away. It forced her to veer to the right and almost collide with Royce Simms in his AeroWing craft. The seconds smeared together as she tried to compose herself, but it proved futile. Olivia put in an average performance and she finished far lower than she expected. Trying to make up time, she had skimmed the air gates twice, adding ten seconds to her finish time. Her sloppy execution was obvious to the spectators, her crew, and herself. She was astonished that she had flown so badly. It devastated Olivia. She knew she had to change her preparation and race strategy if she wanted to improve her performance in Brazil.

SkyRace GP Division 1 Pilot Standings after the South African event. Yellow indicates leader.

Location	Olivia	total	Aleeza	total	Lukas	total
USA	25 (1st)	119	20 (3rd)	129	22 (2nd)	120
Spain	14 (5th)	133	11 (8th)	140	25 (1st)	145
Japan	18 (4th)	151	22 (2nd)	162	12 (7th)	157
Canada	25 (1st)	(151) 176	14 (5th)	176	13 (6th)	170
Saudi Arabia	11 (8th)	187	12 (7th)	188	5 (9th)	175
Egypt	20 (3rd)	207	DNF	188	25 (1st)	200
Mexico	18 (4th)	225	Withdrawn	188	14 (5th)	214
Türkiye	DNF	225	25 (1st) +1	214	13 (6th)	227
South Africa	4 (10th)	229	22 (2nd)	236	12 (7th)	239

'Heading into the final race of the SkyRace GP season here in the undulating sheets of Maranhão sand dunes, east of the city of São Luís, in Brazil,' Katie Kang began, 'local legend and race favourite, Lukas de Castro, will go in leading what is a final race shootout. If the three leading pilots are amped up and pulling the V's, this will go down to the wire and in infamy as one of the most dramatic title deciders we've ever seen in SkyRace history for several reasons. First, we have sisters vying for the title, the Martin sisters, Aleeza and Olivia. Second, the Martin sisters and Lukas de Castro are all within ten points of one another for the pilot's World Championship. Finally, they were almost inseparable during sprint qualifying, with Olivia Martin, Aleeza Martin, and de Castro, all setting down virtually the same time to within milliseconds. Let me explain. They all clocked 14 minutes and 34 seconds, with only milliseconds separating them. Olivia Martin was slowest, on 485 milliseconds, Lukas de Castro on 210 milliseconds and Aleeza Martin came in ahead of them both on 180 milliseconds. They will all start on poll in the front row of the grid. So, we have sisters, the top three pilots on points and unbelievably close qualifying times, all on poll. I have never seen before this. Unprecedented.'

'It certainly is, Katie,' Harvie Stedman continued the commentary on the start grid amongst racepods and crews. 'I love this sky circuit. The hypnotic pattern of the sand dunes punctuated by water is a true natural wonder. The sea breeze makes it just bearable in this warm Brazilian summer. I'm hearing through my comms we are ready to go to the pre-race media conference. Let's take you there.'

Once again, organisers deliberately positioned Lukas de Castro between Aleeza and Olivia in the comfy chairs: He was pumped to start that Q&A session in front of his home crowd as perspiration in the standing-room-only conference room stung the air.

'Welcome,' the MC greeted journalists and the 200 million viewers around the globe. 'We're sorry about the air conditioning issue. A crew is looking into it.' He wiped his brow with his already damp handkerchief. 'The 2048 SkyRace Grand Prix World Championship season comes to its climax in this humid Brazilian summer. Let's just recap where we are on the points standing table after 15 races. Olivia Martin from the Lazzrini Race Team is in third position on 229 points. Aleeza Martin from McRory Racing is in second position on 236 points, and just three points ahead is Lukas de Castro from Eagle One Racing on 239 points. There are just ten points separating these three skilful pilots after 15 races. Brazilian fans are in a frenzy as any of these top points scorers could take out the World Championship title today. Lukas, you are here in front of your home crowd. Is that enough of an advantage?'

'My fans love me here and it's great to see they are out in force to watch their champion take home the World Championship. This was always going to be my year to win, even though some in this room were content with sowing seeds of doubt.'

'First question is from Lois Grattan from Sports Illustrated,' the MC introduced.

A microphone was passed down the line of seated reporters as she stood and took the mic. 'Congratulations to all three of you on where you are today. My question is for Aleeza Martin. You are on track to win a second SkyRace GP World Championship, having podium finishes in your last two starts. Are you confident you'll be the winner today?'

'This has been a tough year. If I can finish on the podium, I'll be thrilled. If I end up winning the World Championship, that will be icing on the cake. A lot can go wrong between now and then. I believe McRory Racing is at the peak of our preparation and we'll win the Team Points Standings for a second year, and that's the important one.'

'Next up is Alex Phillips from Wide World of Sports,' the MC continued.

'My question is for Olivia Martin. There was an earlier report after the sprint qualifying that you had race officials double check the width of your front wing just to be sure things were legal. Can you confirm that?'

Olivia smiled. 'You could say I was a little paranoid. Today is the culmination of the Lazzrini Racing Team's year-long effort. I just wanted to make sure everything was within race regulations.'

'You finished outside the top eight in South Africa,' Alex quickly added. 'You need a podium finish to be in contention today. Are you confident?'

'Alex, if I said I wasn't, I might as well let you fly for me.' The crowd laughed. She considered her sister. 'Alex, I think I can predict there will be a Martin on the podium at the end of the race.'

During the 30-minute walk through before the race, superfans wanting photos and autographs to mark this historic finale, surrounded Lukas de Castro, Olivia and Aleeza. Bayden Turner and Nicolas Martin watched and chatted from the start grid sidelines as the controlled commotion played out. Security personnel and P-droids were interspersed throughout the start grid chaos, on standby to intervene at the slightest hint of unrest as race officials maintained queues. The P-droids exceptional sensory perception and networked communication created a unified surveillance presence that provided spectators, pilots and crews with an added layer of safety.

Reckless mistakes, perhaps nerves, had the three poll position leaders struggling. Everyone knew that one small tactical error could mean the difference between success and failure. By the end of the second lap, both sisters and de Castro had all floundered their advantage. Paul van der Meer from Vogel Machina, Aimee Walton-Dewa from Red Roo and Kawano Takayuki from Hoverflyers flew aggressively during the last SkyRace GP World Championship event. Tens of millions of dollars were equivalent to one place in the Team Points Standings.

By the end of the third lap, Aleeza's racepod had momentarily stalled twice. Something wasn't right. She made an unexpected pit stop and her crew effectively resolved a battery nanacitro connection issue. This cost her valuable time. Aleeza had to finish in the top eight to have any chance of winning the championship. Aleeza's wrist was still not as strong as she'd hoped, and it gave her grief. Clawing her way back against stiff competition under gruelling heat conditions, she sat in tenth position by the seventh lap. She demanded everything from her racepod.

Olivia knew she needed to finish fourth or better to win the championship. She took a deep breath and charged forward with adrenaline coursing through her veins. She was determined to make the most of her opportunity and push herself to the limit. Every second counted, and she didn't intend to let this chance slip away. She knew she was ahead of both Aleeza and Lukas de Castro, but she had to stay there.

On the second last lap, Seo Hye-bin, the #1 pilot for Watson-Cruz, was sitting in fifth position when she clipped the back of the X Force racepod flown by Matilda Vettel. The Watson-Cruz racepod swung to the left before hitting a small dune, ricocheting up and cartwheeling into a surprised group of spectators on a dune 50 metres away. It happened in seconds. The small group scattered in panic as the racepod's front wing, rotor housings and blades broke apart, sending shrapnel and pieces in all directions. The racepod came to rest upside down on its cockpit. As the cockpit airbags deflated and the sandy air settled, Seo Hye-bin lay motionless.

'Accident alert, accident alert, rescue vehicle en route,' the Race Traffic Controller notified all pilots through their helmet comms.

Emergency services arrived quickly, but it was too late for a couple of the spectators. Composite rotor blades with an inlaid titanium leading edge had unfortunately sliced through the head of one and wedged in the middle of the chest of another. Seo Hye-bin and the two remaining injured spectators were treated and taken to hospital as the race continued.

Matilda Vettel's X Force racepod had sustained damage from the incident with Seo Hye-bin and Olivia steadily reeled her in and took her on a tight corner going into the last chicane of the circuit.

Aleeza out manoeuvred Lukas to take up eighth position several hundred metres from the finish. The lead swarm of eight zeroed in on the finish line and thrashed their machines to get there.

Olivia checked her Ghost Pod display for her place.

'You finished fourth!' Henri yelled over the comms. 'Eighteen points should do it!'

'Have I done enough to win?' Olivia thought. 'I hope so.' Relieved, she throttled down and relaxed. She finished the race in front of Aleeza

and Lukas. Olivia felt a sense of achievement and pride in what she had done.

Aleeza checked her interface and confirmed she had finished eighth. 'Where did Olivia finish?' Aleeza asked Gordie.

'Fourth. Eighteen points for her and 11 for you. Both of you have 247 points.'

'Wow,' Aleeza let out a pent-up sigh of relief. She had been dreading the race all week. Last year she was the clear cut leader, this year was never assured. But now that it was over, she felt a weight lifted off her shoulders. She was ready for the off-season to spend time with Bayden.

'Aleeza finished fourth,' Henri told Olivia forlornly. 'You both have 247 points.'

'Fuck!' Olivia punched the cockpit canopy as her effervescence vanished. She closed her eyes and took a deep breath, steeling herself for the encounter ahead. She would have to share the limelight with Aleeza.

'Olivia, this is Sergio. I have something to tell you. Your last lap was the fastest. You picked up the golden point. You have won the World Championship.'

Olivia held her breath for a moment. 'Say again.'

'You have won the World Championship, Olivia,' Sergio repeated slowly, deliberately. 'Congratulations.'

'Yeeesss! Wooooo!' Olivia screamed with delight as she realised this result was exactly what she wanted. Tears of relief rolled down her cheeks. She was overwhelmed with joy and struggled to suppress her emotions. She felt a wave of accomplishment and satisfaction rush through her.

'Olivia picked up the point for the fastest lap,' Gordie broke the news to Aleeza.

'She won,' her small, deflated voice replied. 'Good on her.'

'We won the team points, Aleeza, well done. That's where the money is.'

'It most surely is, Gordie. Bonuses for everyone.'

Landing on the starting grid after the race, Aleeza raised her cockpit canopy. She felt the sun's warmth on her skin and a smile spread across her face. She stood and scanned the grid. The commotion around Olivia was clear. Aleeza caught her eye and gave her a thumbs up with a smile. Olivia considered her sister before returning a two-fingered salute, accompanied by a slight grin.

'Some late news about the spectators fatally injured in the accident earlier. Reports have been filtering through that they were from a German tour group,' Katie Kang informed viewers. 'They were in an approved safety zone but four of them moved to a closer dune inside the high-risk spectator exclusion zone and that smaller group were the spectators injured. Organisers have launched an investigation.'

'A very sad result, Katie, on such a special day,' Harvie Stedman added. 'That unfortunate incident has put a dampener on the last race of the season. Rules are in place to protect spectators, but as we have seen today, reckless choices can have extremely negative consequences. It's important to remember that no matter what, personal safety must always come first.'

SkyRace GP Division 1 Pilot Standings after the Brazilian event. Yellow indicates leader.

Location	Olivia	total	Aleeza	total	Lukas	total
USA	25 (1st)	119	20 (3rd)	129	22 (2nd)	120
Spain	14 (5th)	133	11 (8th)	140	25 (1st)	145
Japan	18 (4th)	151	22 (2nd)	162	12 (7th)	157
Canada	25 (1st)	(151) 176	14 (5th)	176	13 (6th)	170
Saudi Arabia	11 (8th)	187	12 (7th)	188	5 (9th)	175
Egypt	20 (3rd)	207	DNF	188	25 (1st)	200
Mexico	18 (4th)	225	Withdrawn	188	14 (5th)	214
Türkiye	DNF	225	25 (1st) +1	214	13 (6th)	227
South Africa	4 (10th)	229	22 (2nd)	236	12 (7th)	239
Brazil	18 (4th) +1	248	11 (8th)	247	5 (9th)	244

'Joining me on the show tonight is the SkyRace GP superstar, Aleeza Martin,' Stark Green introduced. 'Welcome, Aleeza.' The silver-haired talk show host was known for his wit and charm, as well as his sincere interest in his guests and their stories. Stark had been a fixture in the entertainment industry for decades.

Aleeza's holoprojection was beamed into the London studio from Greenwich. 'Hi, Stark, thank you for having me on your show.'

'Three in the afternoon where you are in Connecticut, right?' Her projection occupied the chair opposite Stark's, on the other side of the designer coffee table.

'That's right, five hours behind you.' Aleeza sat in her Greenwich living room in front of a telepresence scanner. Bayden watched her from behind the device.

'The public idolise SkyRace pilots like rock stars. You are demigods who reach mythical proportions of popularity through your risk-taking and death defying skills on the circuit. How do you cope with that sort of attention?'

'My privacy is paramount, Stark. I try to keep a very low profile off-season and between races.'

'Yes, that was clear when you married Bayden Turner. No one saw that on the horizon.'

'It seemed like the right time to do it, while the media was looking the other way, thinking I was recuperating.'

'I've heard that you dress incognito to avoid being recognised in public. Is that true?'

'I'll neither confirm nor deny that, Stark,' she answered with a cheeky grin. 'I'll keep you all guessing.'

'A different approach to your sister, Olivia. Olivia's story captivated the world, rising from nowhere to become World Champion in virtually half a season and she has spent her off-season in the spotlight celebrating with designer drug-fuelled parties, a new man on her arm each week, she's flourishing in her fame.'

'I know we're only a month into the off-season, but Olivia will have to end her goblin mode soon and focus on the next racing season if she wants to defend her title,' Aleeza argued. 'Or she'll crash and burn everyone who has supported her.'

In an exclusive hotel in Los Angeles, Olivia, a hungover mess, propped up on pillows in a super king-sized bed in a trashed room, a naked man passed out beside her, watched her sister on the wall screen through heavy-lidded, bloodshot eyes. 'You do you, I'll do me,' she whispered to the TV.

'Olivia has said that her glitzy lifestyle is the reward of being the World Champion.'

'Stark, did you get me on the show to discuss my sister?' Aleeza teased with a tilt of her head.

'No, no,' he apologised. 'Well, this year has been massive for SkyRace GP. You started off the season as World Champion, then

Marco Franks from the Lazzrini Race Team had an accident and retired for the season, your sister replaced him, Zetta Minn had a fatal freak accident, Olivia won her debut Division 1 race, you broke your wrist in an odd accident getting out of your racepod after a crash, you got married, you returned just six weeks later and won, Oliva crashed in that same race, there was an accident in the Brazilian GP that killed two in the crowd and finally Olivia won the Pilots World Championship by a single point.' He pretended to pant heavily.

'Yes, Stark, certainly an action packed season.'

'Let's start with how your team finished this year. McRory Racing won the Team Points Standings for the second year.'

'Yes, Stark, we won this year, and I'd just like to give a huge shout-out to the other pilots, Brad Hazzard, Max Schroder and our rookie, Valentina Nemeth.'

'Let's talk about a couple of your colleagues before we talk more about you. Brad Hazzard hasn't had his contract renewed with McRory for next year. He'll be flying for Air Schneider?'

'Yes. Our loss will be Air Schneider's gain. Brad is a brilliant pilot, but pilot rosters change as contracts expire or swaps are negotiated at the end of each season.'

'Even mid-season, like Valentina Nemeth replacing your sister Olivia Martin when she swapped shops to the Lazzrini Race Team. How did that sudden swap of Olivia impact you as a team? Did you have any idea it was coming?'

'Mid-season swaps aren't unusual. SkyRace GP is a business and teams trade pilots for one reason or another. As you said, Marco Franks sustained an injury in an accident off-circuit, which called for an immediate replacement for the rest of the season. Olivia was approached and the rest, as they say, is history. It came as a shock, but as a team, McRory has a deep talent pool and we regrouped. Max was promoted to #1 pilot in Division 2 and Val was brought up from our Division 3 feeder team and we got on with the job of competing, being consistent and winning the Team Points Standings for a second year and $400 million in prize money.'

'For you personally, it must have been a kick in the guts when your sister just ditches the team within 24 hours?'

'This is a multi-billion dollar a year sport, Stark, and I'm only one pilot who has a very limited grasp on the machinations of how all the cogs turn to generate that kind of money. The sports media exploited the storylines about our sibling rivalry and personality differences to generate interest in the sport and outside the sport. I don't take decisions other pilots make as a personal affront. That is their choice based on a business decision, even when it's my sister. Our job is to fly, that's it, nothing more, nothing less. One reason Olivia swapped was because she wouldn't be able to fly Division 1 for McRory until Brad or I vacated the pilot roster.'

'So, now that McRory Racing has dropped Brad Hazzard, do you think they might offer Olivia a contract to replace him now that she's World Champion?'

Olivia was only half listening, half watching the wall screen. She was distracted by the array of chaotic thoughts flashing into her head, then scattering. It seemed impossible for her to focus. She took a deep breath to calm the storm inside her mind. Closing her eyes, she pictured a soothing and peaceful environment. She forced herself to concentrate and salvage her thoughts.

Aleeza laughed. 'Well, if the media reports are anything to go by, her extracurricular activities since becoming World Champion may tarnish her credibility and reputation. Team principals and owners take their image very seriously. I don't think I'll see her name on the McRory pilot roster next year. Her party pilot alter ego might prove difficult for some teams to tolerate.'

'Is it hard to go through such a public falling out with your sister, your best friend?'

'It's not something I chose to do, Stark. That was Olivia's course of action. Let's leave it at that.'

'Now, the investigation on Marco Franks' accident that led to his mid-season retirement has concluded, and the final report was leaked to the media. The report accuses deliberate foul play as the cause of the accident. Does that shock you?'

'It doesn't shock me, Stark, it disturbs me. There are undesirable elements in professional sports. We know that, especially sports where so much money is changing hands. It's disturbing and unfortunate that Machiavellian tactics take place in our sport.'

'Who do you think might be behind such malicious tactics that deliberately disrupt the sport by injuring pilots?'

'I have no comment on that, Stark, I don't aim to be next. As I said, this is a massive sport and thousands upon thousands of people rely on it for income, directly or indirectly, so that suspect list would be quite long.'

'You are signed with McRory Racing until the end of the 2050 season, it that right?'

'Yes, Stark. I'll be back on the podium next season and I have my sights set on the 2049 SkyRace GP World Championship.' Aleeza threw down the gauntlet.

᠁d the proclamation with a vacant expression. A knock ⁣or severed her connection with the screen. She ⁣d towards the door and studied the tiny screen ⁣sly opened the door.

'Hello, Olivia,' Jericho Starling greeted with a beaming smile. 'This is Paul Mason-Stuart,' he gestured to the man who stood beside him. Gordie peered at her from behind the shoulders of the pair.

End

More SkyRacers information
can be found on the SkyRacers website:
https://www.skyracers.net
Next novel in the SkyRacers series:
SkyRacers '49 (Book 2)
Dream Phaze
www.dreamphaze.com[1]
Contact
hello@dreamphaze.com

Next novel in the Dream Phaze series:
Dream Phaze – Fascination (Book 3)

---

1. http://www.dreamphaze.com

www.ingramcontent.com/pod-product-compliance
Lightning Source LLC
Chambersburg PA
CBHW020319130626
46549CB00003B/935